DREAD RECKONING

The Bayou Hauntings
Book Nine

Bill Thompson

Published by
Ascendente Books
Dallas, Texas

Books by Bill Thompson

Mysterious America
SERPENT
MIDNIGHT PASS

The Bayou Hauntings
CALLIE
FORGOTTEN MEN
THE NURSERY
BILLY WHISTLER
THE EXPERIMENTS
DIE AGAIN
THE PROCTOR HALL HORROR
THE ATONEMENT
DREAD RECKONING

Brian Sadler Archaeological Mystery Series
THE BETHLEHEM SCROLL
ANCIENT: A SEARCH FOR THE LOST CITY
OF THE MAYAS
THE STRANGEST THING
THE BONES IN THE PIT
ORDER OF SUCCESSION
THE BLACK CROSS
TEMPLE
THE IRON DOOR

Apocalyptic Fiction
THE OUTCASTS

The Crypt Trilogy
THE RELIC OF THE KING
THE CRYPT OF THE ANCIENTS
GHOST TRAIN

Middle Grade Fiction
THE LEGEND OF GUNNERS COVE

THE LAST CHRISTMAS

You'll meet Simba in these pages as Landry Drake and Cate Adams decide to adopt a dog. This book is dedicated to the two people who rescued Simba and brought him into our lives...and by extension, into the lives of Landry and Cate.

My stepson Cory and his girlfriend Paola found an abandoned puppy in a box. Consummate animal lovers, they brought him home and cared for him, and he ultimately became our dog. Paola named him Simba because he was brave and strong.

Cory tragically died a few months later, and Paola, who lives in Mexico, hasn't seen Simba since he was a puppy. But she'll be back, little boy, and you'll be thrilled to see the girl who loves you so much.

Thanks to Cory and Paola for bringing us another four-legged bundle of enthusiasm and love!

CHAPTER ONE

The French Quarter is haunted. It's a fact the residents accept, the tourists make nervous jokes about, and city officials encourage so long as it doesn't affect the visitors who spend millions of dollars in the Big Easy every year. Supernatural events started in the Quarter centuries ago, when ships came to New Orleans, then America's largest port, bringing goods from all over the world, including humans snatched from their homes in Africa and the Caribbean islands. It seemed God turned a blind eye to the auctions in front of St. Louis Cathedral, but the customs, rituals, and secrets these imprisoned souls knew transformed New Orleans into a town like no other. The craft had many names—voodoo or juju or witchcraft or black magic—and it wasn't taken lightly because the supernatural flourished in New Orleans then. Today, three hundred years later, nothing has changed.

———

As dusk settled over the enchanting streets of the French Quarter, Angie Bovida, an intrepid traveler from Mississippi whose interests ranged from Southern culture to the paranormal, walked resolutely along the narrow streets until she reached the one she sought, a quiet street called Dauphine nestled deep in the heart of the Quarter.

Bourbon Street had all the noise and sex and partying, but Dauphine Street, just one block away, had none of the craziness for which the French Quarter was famous. Instead, it was home to boutique hotels, cozy local bars, and eclectic shops sandwiched between some of the city's oldest homes. Majestic at one time, today most were aging behemoths that owners were reluctant to sink money into.

Angie found the house she was looking for, a rambling three-story mansion in the 800 block that was a relic of bygone eras. The guidebook in her pocket—*Dark Secrets of New Orleans*—described the structure, known as Tartarus House and erected in 1723 by a wealthy indigo planter named Moros, as "a genuinely haunted building, a hotbed of supernatural activity on almost any night of the year and a frightening place. Locals claim to have seen eerie apparitions and heard horrific screams of terror when walking past the house. People have reported such strange feelings that they switch to the other side of the street when walking down that block. This one is not for the faint of heart." Once Angie read those words—powerful ones to be posted in a guidebook—she was determined to go there and get inside.

The book dedicated several pages to the home and its history. Imposing and grand ages ago, today the ancient house stood in ruin, its crumbling plaster exposing brick, giving a glimpse into layers of its past. It had served several roles; in the early eighteen hundreds it became a home for "wayward girls," the euphemism for pregnant, unmarried teens whose mortified parents relegated them to a "home." By 1830 it was an orphanage, and after the Yankees captured the city in 1862, a Union general named Abner McJunkin moved his staff in with the children and made it his headquarters. He left a year later, but the orphans stayed until 1890. Afterwards, the old place sat empty, descending into decay while appearing more and more like the haunted mansion people swore it to be.

It became part of travel guides, ghost tours, and books about the supernatural. Passersby claimed the grotesque plaster statues in the front yard swayed and turned in the darkness, eerie lights appeared in the windows, and horrifying shrieks and groans emanated through broken windowpanes far up on the top floor. College students made the short walk from Bourbon Street to see the infamous house, daring each other to spend an hour inside or, if sufficiently fueled by alcohol, the entire night. The guidebook didn't mention if anyone did so or what might have happened.

The Civil War general who lived there with his staff for more than a year wrote a book about his experiences. Besides the guidebook *Dark Secrets*, Angie Bovida had bought General McJunkin's book and discovered she shouldn't read it in bed because his vivid descriptions gave her nightmares. The officer, a pragmatic man not given to exaggeration or tall tales, wrote of terrifying things— specters rising from the earth in the front yard, eerie, opaque figures floating through doors during the night, and many other horrifying, unexplainable encounters. His experiences gave credence to the guidebook's claim that the old mansion was a hotbed of supernatural activity.

Angie thought of those things as she stood on Dauphine Street, looking at the house she'd read so much about. *Yes, it seems forbidding and scary*, she told herself, *but so would any house that sat vacant and unkept for more than a hundred years.*

A picket fence that had once been white surrounded a weed-filled garden, their tendrils entwining around a post to which a sign was affixed. *Tartarus House.* The unfamiliar name meant nothing to her; perhaps it belonged to the last occupant or the original owner.

The house creaked with each passing breeze, as if sighing under the weight of the things that had taken place within its walls. It was one of the oldest structures in the French Quarter, an area with a deep, dark past of its own. Things happened on these ancient streets that weren't understood then, and no feats of modern technology could explain them now.

She was certain the macabre house had secrets of its own and that it was empty. Who would live in such a place, with jagged shards of glass in the windowpanes, a rotting porch, and darkness within? The Moros family, the original owners, had to be long gone, and that suited Angie, because a part of her wanted to go into the house that seemed to watch her with a haunting stillness.

An overpowering sense of dread swept over her. The ancient mansion stood like a towering dead thing, and it scared the hell out of her. Perhaps it was her own heart pounding with anxiety and trepidation, but she swore the house was pulsing as though it were a living thing.

I shouldn't do this. I'm perfectly fine out here, and I can say I've seen the house. It's probably locked anyway, and in the dark I might fall through a hole in the floor. She enumerated these logical reasons she should walk away, but she shrugged off her terror and mustered the courage to push ahead.

Unbeknownst to Angie, supernatural forces were set into motion when she ignored a "KEEP OUT" sign, pushed a rotting gate aside, and meandered through the overgrown foliage that cast eerie shadows on the decaying facade. A sense of foreboding washed over her as she stumbled through the gnarled stems of unkempt bushes pushing skyward, as if desperate to reach the light.

Where once there had been lavish flower beds and manicured hedges, now the air hung heavy with the scent of damp earth and decay. She approached the house, its warped wooden siding and broken windows testaments to years of neglect. She heard the sagging porch creaking—whispering, perhaps—even before she climbed the rotting stairs. An ancient porch swing, frozen in time, swung casually back and forth, although there was no breeze to cause it to do so.

The moment she entered the gloom that hung over the dilapidated veranda, everything safe, sane and predictable took a pause. Shadows created macabre shapes that Angie sensed were following her with unseen eyes as she took tentative steps to stand before the ancient, weathered front door. She took a deep breath, somehow feeling that the house was doing the same, inhaling slowly as it waited for someone daring enough to tackle its chilling secrets and haunting tales within.

Once a grand entrance, today the faded door was a pale, ghostly shade of gray, and she gasped when she tried the knob and the door creaked open.

How can it be unlocked? Anyone could come in and ransack the house.

She allowed herself a nervous chuckle at that silly thought. The place was a total wreck, and no amount of ransacking could make it worse. Shivering with anticipation and fear, she stepped inside, departing the world she understood and entering the realm of the unknown.

CHAPTER TWO

On the same night Angie visited the house on Dauphine Street, a series of eerie and unnerving events began. The evening was thick with the intoxicating energy of Mardi Gras in New Orleans. Crowds of revelers roamed the streets, their laughter and music blending in with the lively chaos that defined the city's most famous celebration. But this Carnival season would begin on a sinister note; in the house Angie Bovida visited, plans were underway to disrupt the merrymaking and unleash fear and confusion among the thousands who gathered in the Big Easy.

It was a Friday ten days before Mardi Gras, the same night that the first downtown parades of Carnival season rolled down St. Charles Avenue. Over the coming days, people would realize that what had seemed like random acts were part of a pattern. Odd things happened at first, but before it ended, they would become horrifying and deadly. Early on, shopkeepers, servers, and hotel employees dependent on tourist dollars spoke of the unsettling events only in whispers. It was important for tourists to believe everything was fine—that scary events were not unheard of in the Big Easy. People began calling them the Harbingers—the omens or signs of things to come. Signs of what, nobody knew.

In the weeks after Mardi Gras ended, folks would recall that the first inexplicable event happened at the Krazy Kat Klub on Bourbon Street. Four men in their twenties— workers from an offshore Gulf rig enjoying a weekend off—sat at a bar that abutted the stage, sipping beers while watching a naked, disinterested stripper named Lotta Love do her thing. The atmosphere in the dimly lit bar was tinged with an air of curiosity and unease as patrons took their eyes off Miss Love to steal glances at a peculiar figure seated in a corner. An odd man, out of place in a strip club, captured the attention of those who noticed him.

The long, flowing cloak he wore cascaded to the floor, the bar's ambient lighting causing the fabric to glow with an iridescent sheen. It was adorned with patterns reminiscent of ancient runes and symbols, hinting at a mysterious origin or purpose.

Perched upon the strange man's head was a tall, pointed black hat adorned with the same mysterious symbols. Its tip reached toward the ceiling, as if bridging the gap between this world and the realm of the supernatural. In one hand he held a slender golden stick that glimmered when the light hit it. What might have been bizarrely odd in, say, Pittsburgh barely warranted a second glance in the Big Easy during Mardi Gras, when thousands of people walked about in costumes far more garish than his.

As they stole glances, the young rig workers sensed that this was no Carnival reveler. His ageless countenance and untouched beer gave the impression of a man at the same time evil and wise, one who bore the weight of unspoken secrets, a creepy, slightly scary misfit sitting alone in a Bourbon Street bar, wearing a magician's outfit. When one guy wondered aloud why a weirdo would choose a titty bar to while away his time, the man turned his head and stared at him, his eyes seemingly piercing into the young man's thoughts. Embarrassed, he averted his eyes.

"With all this noise, he couldn't have heard me," he said as his nervous friends admonished him, and he was right. The music was amped up to an ear-splitting level so that a hawker out on Bourbon Street could entice tourists to come see the raunchiest show in town for a two-drink minimum of watered-down whisky.

"What the hell's he doing now?" one asked, pointing at the strange man, who raised the golden stick—the wand, as they later described it to the police—high above his head and mouthed silent words. Suddenly he stood and screamed a single word—*Moros!*—that resonated above the cacophony, causing even Lotta Love to stop her pole dance and look, and then a huge puff of white smoke enveloped him. When it dissipated, there was only an empty barstool and an untouched Abita Amber.

Several screaming patrons made for the door while the naked Miss Love darted off the stage. The bartender grabbed a fire extinguisher, but it was useless; within seconds, like the mysterious man, the cloud of smoke disappeared.

At the same time and just a few blocks away, the Central Business District pulsed with the sounds of celebration. On this warm late February evening in New Orleans, music came from all directions as the first downtown Mardi Gras parades of the season made their way down St. Charles Avenue. The one honoring the Krewe of Oshun led the way with twenty-eight floats lumbering onto Canal Street around eight p.m., followed by the Krewes of Cleopatra and Alla. Arms outstretched, thousands of spectators cried out for trinkets, and the men and women high up on the massive floats gave their fans what they wanted, tossing beads and doubloons and souvenir cups into their outstretched hands.

The krewes that organized and funded the Carnival

parades spent tens of thousands of dollars and a year of work on ornately designed and decorated floats featuring larger-than-life sculptures, intricate artwork and themed displays. Krewe members who rode on the floats wore elaborate, colorful costumes and masks, and between the massive moving platforms marched high school bands and local musical groups playing upbeat New Orleans jazz. Spectators, many dressed in their own festive attire, danced to the music as they cried out to the riders standing on the floats high above them. "Throw me somethin', mistuh!" was the cry, answered by showers of colorful beads, small toys, and souvenir plastic coins marked with the year and name of the krewe. Catching the throws was a cherished tradition, and people engaged in friendly competition to see who could bag the most items.

There were twenty-two massive floats in this evening's third and last parade, Alla, but when what should have been the final float made the right turn from St. Charles Avenue onto Canal, a hush fell over the crowd. Somehow, somewhere along the parade route, a twenty-third float had mysteriously appeared at the end of the procession. A tall float draped in black stood in stark contrast to the brightly colored ones. Tall flambeaux on each corner sent flames high into the air and added to an aura of mystery that seemed to engulf the riders and the robed man in a tall, pointed hat, who sat on a black throne at the summit of the moving structure. His robe and hat glistened with mysterious symbols, and in his right hand he waved a golden wand from the tip of which sparks flew like a Fourth of July sparkler. He was dressed as some kind of sorcerer, spectators thought as they drew back in fear when the float passed by them.

Ghostly riders dressed in tattered clothing leered at the crowds, their faces twisted in malevolent rage. Throwing no trinkets, they stared intently into the faces of expectant tourists looking for goodies. The crowd was terrified at the sight; many began to scream and push backward to distance themselves from the eerie float. Chaos ensued as revelers were trampled in the melee, and police who ran to the scene were helpless against a mob terrified by a Mardi Gras float.

Ignoring the mayhem, the float silently moved on. A sense of unease and an eerie quietness swept over the teeming crowd as the ominous twelve-foot-tall black float glided by, pulled by a tractor bearing a sign.

Krewe of Moros. The Harbinger of Doom.

Locals looked at each other in surprise. *Krewe of Moros? What the hell was that?* No one had heard of it, nor was it on any of the parade schedules posted online. And only one float? No krewe went to the time and expense of entering a parade with only one float. The eerie figure on the float was called the Harbinger of Doom…the precursor of ominous things to come.

The aura of mystery took a surprising twist when the parade turned off Canal Street for its final few blocks down Tchoupitoulas to the spot where the floats would stop and the riders disembark. Only a few people stood on the sidewalks there; Mardi Gras devotees knew there'd be nothing left to toss out. Once the floats departed the wide avenue for a narrow, dark street, the men and women who'd been throwing beads and doubloons were unmasking, swigging drinks from flasks and preparing for the after-parties to follow.

That meant only a few die-hard people on the sidewalk watched as the lone float of the nonexistent Krewe of Moros rounded the corner and vanished into the darkness.

Literally.

CHAPTER THREE

As other unusual events unfolded in the days leading up to Mardi Gras itself, the hotline at the Paranormal Network received dozens of calls a day instead of the usual four or five a week. Cate Adams, the office manager for TPN, listened to them all, deleting most while archiving the few that seemed interesting. More frustrating was the steady stream of visitors who appeared unannounced at the network's offices on Toulouse Street, hoping to see the famous Landry Drake and find out his take on the mysterious occurrences.

Since starting the network two years ago with his girlfriend, Cate, and his good friend and mentor Henri Duchamp, people recognized Landry Drake wherever he went. His popular documentaries on supernatural occurrences in Louisiana and the South were eagerly anticipated by millions across the country, and the paranormal hotline, installed when the fledgling network needed fodder for its shows, had become the way avid viewers could report unusual events and sightings in hopes they'd appear on television.

"Landry, come listen for a sec," Cate called across the open space that was the network's office. When he came to her office door, she played a message.

They listened to a female's voice, anxious and hesitant. "Er, this is…well, it doesn't matter. This isn't about me. My daughter is missing, and I wonder if it's part of that supernatural stuff going on in the French Quarter. Her name's Angie. Angie Bovida. She's thirty-eight and lives with me in Gulfport, and she watches all of Landry Drake's unexplained mystery shows. I know she's in New Orleans, because she called me on Friday to say she was going to check out a haunted house somewhere in the French Quarter. I get a call from her every morning and night without fail, but I didn't hear from her all weekend. Something's wrong, Mr. Drake. Please help me!" She left a number and disconnected.

"You know how it is in our city," Landry said as he turned away. "People get a little distracted here. Booze, partying, Mardi Gras parades—they forget to call Mommy and check in. Now that strange phenomena are making the national news, it's only going to get worse."

Cate shook her head. "The girl's thirty-eight years old; she's not a kid. And the mother sounds frantic. I'm going to call her back."

"Tell her to call the police. It's not our job to look for a missing person." He crossed the room to his cubicle, turned back, and yelled, "On second thought, don't call her back. We don't have time to waste on this." Then he slammed the door, rattling its frame.

Typically laid-back, the recent events weighed so heavily on Landry that those close to him noticed a change in his demeanor. Everyone expected him to understand and interpret the supernatural, but the Harbingers defied imagination in both their frequency and intensity. He grew irritable and sullen and began taking his frustration out on his best friends Cate and Henri.

Alone in his office, he stared out the window, trying to make sense of everything. Vanishing people and a phantom parade float that didn't exist but was seen by thousands—what the hell was going on? People considered him an expert on the paranormal and gravitated to him for help, but this time he was the one seeking answers. He leaned back in his chair, put his feet on the desk, and massaged his temples.

By midafternoon, the stream of visitors milling about their office had become a never-ending flow of faces and voices that interrupted every attempt Landry made to do something productive. Unaware—or unconcerned—about their disrespectful behavior, visitors would stare through the glass into his office and give a brief rap on the pane. When he looked up and glared at them, they waved and beat a hasty retreat.

"It's like they're trying to get the gorilla's attention at the zoo," he grumbled to himself, and after the fourth such encounter, he buzzed Cate, telling her they had to stop this stream of people. "Lock the door downstairs," he suggested, but she believed they had a right to come to the network and promised to deal with them. And she tried, but every time one left, two more ascended the stairs and strolled around the open-air office area, poking their heads into everything and pushing Landry to the brink. For a while he attempted to remain composed and professional, but the constant interruptions at last pushed him over. He couldn't work or think or make a call. Laptop under his arm, he opened his office door, and without a glance in either direction, he strode across the room, dodged visitors, and took the stairs up to the studio on the third floor. The door at the bottom of the stairs bore an "Authorized Personnel Only" sign, which Landry hoped would work.

On the third floor he would be free from the steady stream of visitors who milled about the office, hoping to corner him and get his take on the Harbingers. In concept he understood; people rarely came to the network, but many were becoming frightened. But he had nothing to give them, and he had ended up trapped in his own office while strangers peeked through the window to see inside. He was getting nothing done anyway—his mind careened from one bizarre mystery to another as he struggled for answers—but at least on the third floor he found solitude while Cate dealt with the throng of uninvited guests.

The Harbingers. Landry considered it a fitting name for the unsettling mysteries that had been happening. Maybe that was what they were—dark omens foretelling things to come, events that would disrupt Mardi Gras day and affect the millions of celebrants who would pack New Orleans for the occasion. Harbingers or not, they had been frightening, and for Landry, two things were probable. These were paranormal events, and they were only the beginning.

Killing time, he searched the web for the phrase *Harbingers and New Orleans*, and he perked up when he saw something interesting. This wasn't the first time a series of unexplainable events happened. In 1923, one hundred years ago, Mardi Gras festivities were disrupted by pop-up storms; tall, masked figures in long robes crashed parties and appeared and disappeared on floats as they rolled along the parade routes; and nearly naked, garishly painted men and women engaged in voodoo rituals at the gates of St. Louis Cemetery, terrifying residents and tourists alike.

Back then, locals called them misfortunes, but a *Times-Picayune* reporter referred to them using the word *harbingers*—portents or omens of things to come. Although the events had been forgotten over time, Landry found it intriguing that the odd name was being used again this year.

He finished reading the article and turned away, but looked back when his eye caught another search engine response. The article was in French, but despite not speaking the language, he understood the date, February 23, 1823, and the title—*Les Harbingers à la Nouvelle Orléans*. He pasted the article into a translation program and read the story from a long-defunct newspaper called *Le Courrier de la Louisiane* about yet another Carnival season disrupted by a series of terrifying and unexplainable events. And it had happened two hundred years ago.

History had repeated itself every hundred years since 1823. Hoping for more, Landry searched for news from a century earlier, learning that Mardi Gras had in fact been celebrated in the settlement of New Orleans in 1723, but nothing specific from the period existed on the web.

His thoughts turned to the phantom float that had materialized at the end of the downtown parades, only to disappear soon thereafter. It bore the name "Harbinger of Doom," and at its very top had stood a mysterious masked figure named Moros. Unfamiliar with the name, Landry searched the web. It was a European surname that was also a nickname meaning foolish or stupid.

There was another more sinister meaning, one much closer to the point of what was happening in New Orleans. Moros was a Greek god, the offspring of Erebus, god of darkness, and Nyx, evil goddess of night. His brothers were the dark gods of the underworld.

Moros could give people the ability to see their own deaths. Hated and feared by mortals, he was responsible for those tingling, scary feelings that foretold some terrible fate. Death or violence, illness or destruction—these were the places to which Moros, the harbinger of doom, enticed humans.

At 3:30 Cate messaged, summoning him downstairs to her office. As he stepped into the room, he was surprised to see only a few strangers still there. A woman sat in Cate's cubicle, dabbing at her eyes with a tissue while talking nonstop. Landry paused at the door, watched for a moment, and gave Cate a questioning shrug. He hoped this wasn't the reason she'd called him, but Cate gestured to him and said, "Carolyn Bovida, meet Landry Drake."

After leaving her voicemail asking Landry for help, the distraught mother of the missing Angie Bovida had driven from Gulfport to New Orleans in hopes she could meet the famous ghost hunter and convince him to help. It was her good fortune that she ended up speaking to Cate, who sympathized with a mother's plight and insisted Landry come listen to her story.

"Ma'am, I'm sorry about your daughter—" he began, but that was as far as he got before Cate interrupted.

"Landry, I told Mrs. Bovida you would listen to her and give her some advice about the situation. That's the least we can do after she made the effort—"

He snapped, "No, Cate, because that isn't what we do. Mrs. Bovida, our work is with the paranormal. From your message, I gather your daughter was going to what she thought was a haunted house. With all respect, hundreds of buildings in New Orleans—perhaps thousands—are considered haunted. Tourists love the concept, and having a drink in a spooky bar or dinner in a haunted restaurant brings in the dollars. There's nothing to indicate—"

The woman began to cry, and Cate snapped, "Stop it, Landry. Sit down and listen to her for a minute." The harsh command and a finger pointing to a chair was all it took. Landry sat like an obedient dog.

CHAPTER FOUR

"My daughter has always been different," Carolyn Bovida explained to Landry and Cate. "She's a sweet girl, still lives at home at thirty-eight, and hasn't been lucky at holding down jobs or finding a man. I don't know what I'd do without her, but sometimes she gets on these fixation binges, and I can't stop her from following them through until she gets frustrated and gives up."

"She came to New Orleans by herself, correct?" Landry asked, and the lady nodded. "I don't mean to pry into your business, but if I'm going to help, I need to understand a few things. How did she get here? Does she have a source of income, or did you pay her way?"

"Angie gets a disability check, and we consider that her money. She doesn't chip in on the rent or expenses or any of that, but she helps around the house when I ask her to. She's a good girl—"

Landry interrupted. "Let's try to stay on topic, Mrs. Bovida." Cate frowned, but he ignored her. If he was going to be roped into talking with this lady, at least he was going to find out as much as he could. "How did Angie get here? Did she come from Gulfport?"

"Yes, on the bus. And she said she was going to stay at a hostel near the French Quarter. Thirty-nine dollars a day, she said. Bunk beds and roommates. Not my cup of tea, that's for sure, but if you're broke, I guess it works."

Landry found out Angie had a debit card that was tied to her mother's bank account. He asked her to check recent charges to see if they could locate the hostel and speak to someone there. "So you're going to help me?" she cried. "Thank God!"

"I didn't say that, and it's too early to know if I can get involved." He said he'd do enough investigating to find out if there was a paranormal aspect to the story. Her statement that Angie was going to check out a haunted house was the only hook, and if that didn't pan out soon, he'd have to let the authorities do the looking, since it was their job, after all. "Speaking of which," he added, "why haven't you spoken to the police?"

"Because Angie's afraid of them. She's been...well, committed, I guess you'd say, more than once. Sometimes she's gotten out of hand and had to be restrained. She...uh, she bit a police officer once, and he tased her and taped her mouth shut until they got her to a psychiatric facility. It was traumatic for her and me both, but I guess it was necessary."

"Has Angie ever disappeared?" Cate asked, and she nodded. "She's gotten mad at me a few times and run away. But she always came back."

"What's the longest she was ever gone?" Landry asked.

"Almost three months, one time two years ago."

"Three months?" Incredulous, he looked at Cate and shook his head. "Mrs. Bovida, I'm sorry, but there's no way I'm getting involved in this. There's no proof anything at all happened to your daughter. She's a grown woman. She may be off somewhere doing whatever she wants, and she likely will turn back up like she always has before. This isn't something we do, nor do we have the time. You need to call the police."

He stood, thanked her for coming, and walked out. Cate did nothing to stop him, and a few minutes later, she came to his office. "She left, Landry, and I apologize. I felt sorry for her, but I have to agree with you. Angie most likely isn't in trouble; she's just off doing her own thing. You gave her some good advice, and maybe her mother can check the debit card charges and find Angie herself. You're exactly right; with all these supernatural phenomena going on, we don't have time to look for her."

At the same time and just a half mile away, Angie Bovida sat on a cot in a dimly lit five-by-seven-foot room. Wrapping her arms about herself in the blackness of her makeshift prison, she wondered if anyone might be looking for her. She had told no one where she was going—a big mistake, she now realized—but she hoped and prayed that somebody somewhere had figured out she was missing.

And that they'd come in time.

CHAPTER FIVE

Stunned by phenomena no one could explain, the police investigated each incident. They talked to a woman from Mississippi whose daughter had gone missing after saying she was going to visit a haunted house. They took copious notes as people in a bar described a man dressed as a magician who raised a wand and disappeared in a puff of smoke. And many on-duty cops had witnessed the mysterious black float that appeared at the end of a Mardi Gras parade, terrifying some revelers and causing a stampede on Canal Street before disappearing into thin air.

They would return to the precinct station on Royal Street, compare notes to decide if the seemingly unrelated events might be related after all, and come away with nothing except the possibilities of mass hysteria along the parade route, a magic disappearing act in a bar, and a grown woman who might have dropped out of sight to get out of the clutches of an overbearing mother.

The most the cops could hope for was for things to blow over, but what happened was just the opposite. Over the next ten days the mysterious phenomena happened again and again. Small things one day and more significant ones another, but as Mardi Gras Day approached, the manifestations became stronger and more malevolent. Each of them occurred inside the French Quarter or within a few blocks of it, leaving eyewitnesses shaken and scared and filled with tales almost too fanciful to believe.

Visitors who signed up for a ghost tour got their money's worth as they stood outside an old house on Burgundy Street. A guide whose name badge read Zombie Charlie began a canned spiel about a certain frigid night in the dead of winter, when a specter would appear on the roof and jump to her death three stories below. The legend of an enslaved girl imprisoned by her master and finding freedom by taking her own life had been reported as true by several persons over two centuries, but the guide didn't believe a word of it until that recent balmy night not in winter but in spring, when the poor girl appeared and plunged to her death right before the astonished group of tourists, causing the guide, Zombie Charlie, to faint dead away.

It didn't surprise locals to learn that St. Louis Cemetery No. 1, an ancient graveyard reputed to be the burial spot of voodoo queen Marie Laveau, was becoming a hotbed of activity. Moans and groans could be heard on Rampart Street two blocks away, and a pair of matronly women from England, who had no reason to lie, reported turning a corner among the crowded grave markers to find an eerie apparition floating close enough to touch. They ran away screaming bloody murder, and officials padlocked the iron gates to keep the spirits in and the curious out.

Unfortunately, that tactic didn't work. Residents of Basin Street just opposite the main entrance watched as spirits floated in the air outside the fence and even drifted into traffic. Several auto accidents occurred when drivers jerked their wheels to avoid hitting persons standing in the street...who promptly vanished seconds later.

The old cemetery attracted others—the foolhardy who ignored words of caution from locals. A group of boys from Loyola University waited until midnight, approached the barred entrance, and vaulted over. Once inside the graveyard, they found an otherworldly stillness and watched ominous presences float out from behind dozens of tombstones. Flashlights were of no use, they died the moment the spirits approached, and as the boys took refuge inside a crumbling mausoleum bearing the family name MOROS, clouds obscured the waning moon. The hapless intruders were left in darkness as dozens of whirling things flew from the crypt, terrifying even the bravest among them. Shaken but alive, all the college students except one escaped unscathed to relate their horrifying story.

Channel Nine senior investigative reporter Jack Blair opened that evening's newscast with a harrowing sequel to an already terrifying event. During their trespass at the cemetery, one of the boys inside the ancient crypt had dared to go further inside than the rest. He'd maneuvered through a rusty door that slammed shut behind hIm, trapping him for hours among rotting caskets with what he claimed was a bloody, headless corpse. He would emerge with his hair turned snowy white and spend the rest of his life confined to a psychiatric facility. A lighthearted, daring college student when their escapade began, he ended up a pitiful, withdrawn creature whose screams echoed down the hallways of the institution every midnight.

These events and others—the Harbingers—created a pre-Mardi Gras week like no other. Tourists grew wary, and residents became so unsettled that they refused to venture out to parties and parades or to join the raucous activities in the French Quarter.

The supernatural occurrences—for within days everyone accepted that was what they were—devastated the tourism industry, one of New Orleans's biggest sources of revenue. To ensure a safe and happy Mardi Gras, six months earlier the mayor had created a special task force on crime, using vice squad officers to crack down on scams, pickpockets, three-card monte shysters, and other such misdemeanors. Felonies too, because the murder rate in the city had skyrocketed, and this Mardi Gras season there were more cops in the French Quarter and along the parade routes than ever before.

Tartarus House, an old mansion on Dauphine Street, came to the attention of the task force when a disgruntled neighbor complained that the house and yard were in such awful shape that it created an eyesore on the otherwise well-kept block. "There's also strange stuff going on there," the neighbor added. "Nobody comes and goes, the place has been vacant for years, but sometimes there are lights passing by the upstairs windows. Or a weird moaning sound. Probably vagrants who broke in to do fentanyl or something," he grumbled. "How about the city sends somebody to check it out?"

Two veteran beat cops were dispatched to the address. The allegations of strange happenings didn't faze them; their job was to find out if trespassers were inside and if a cleanup citation should be issued. The dispatch order listed the name of the property owner as Bezaliel Moros. One of the officers commented on the odd name, and the other said he probably came here from Europe.

Unaware that Angie Bovida had disappeared in this house two days earlier, the burly cops stood on the sidewalk outside the old gate and surveyed the house that lay far back across an eerie garden. They passed through the gate, ducking and weaving through thick, tangled vegetation overgrown with thorny vines that seemed to writhe and slither in the dim light. One cursed as a thorny bush snagged his department-issued khaki slacks, ripping a two-inch hole.

"This place is effin' weird," one commented as he passed an ancient statue, its eroded features creating a sentinel, faceless but for a pair of piercing, angry eyes that seemed to follow the intruders who had dared venture into the haunting mists of the garden.

They maneuvered through the clinging vines and reached the porch, where one rapped hard on the door, shouted, "POLICE!" and jumped back in surprise when it slowly creaked open. He peeked inside and said, "Nobody there. Musta not been latched. Let's take a look inside."

The other officer stood transfixed on the porch, staring into the parlor that lay beyond the doorway. Both had seen it all, but there was something about Tartarus House that gave them the jitters. Regardless, they had a job to do, and they stepped across the threshold into a dusty front room.

The air was thick with the scent of abandonment. The floorboards groaned as the men moved about, flailing their arms to move ancient cobwebs that clung to their faces. "Police! Anybody home?" one cop yelled, and a mournful groan emanated from somewhere deep in the old mansion. "Did you…uh, hear that?" he whispered.

His partner nodded, and his voice trembled. "It's nothing, I guess. These old houses make sounds all the time."

They saw tattered remnants of peeling wallpaper, the patterns faded and hardly recognizable. Pieces of furniture, once elegant and regal, now lay in pieces, mere skeletons of their former glory. A long-forgotten rocking chair sat by a decaying fireplace at the far end of the room, and a dirt-encrusted portrait of a somber man wearing a top hat hung askew over the mantel.

The cops moved slowly down a hall to the back of the house, where they found shelves and racks filled with things related to magic—robes and books and potions and the like—but without a warrant and seeing nothing illegal, they left things alone.

The older cop, a sergeant close to retirement, walked through a doorway into a dark dining room. Eight rotting chairs stood like soldiers around a long table onto which an intricate chandelier had fallen, breaking into hundreds of tiny glass prisms that reflected what few rays of sunlight filtered through the grimy windowpanes past heavy curtains that hung in shreds.

As his eyes adjusted to the gloom, he noticed something across the room and cursed in surprise. Beside a ruined china cabinet stood an eerie figure in a flowing black robe, its face hidden by a dark gauzy veil. "Leave!" it moaned. "Leave!" The voice was high-pitched and tonal. *Like a woman's,* he thought.

The cop in the other room called out, "Sarge, you okay?"

The eerie figure floated around the dining table toward the sergeant, who backed away and drew his service revolver. "Uh, I think I need help," he cried. "Stop! Hold it right there!" The presence paused just a few feet away, raised an arm, and pointed a slender gold stick in his direction.

The other cop rushed in as the sergeant dropped his weapon and collapsed in a heap on the moth-eaten carpet. "Get away from him!" he shouted to the ghostly figure, who hovered over the sergeant for a few seconds before vanishing.

"I'm calling for backup!" He reached for his radio, but the sergeant, embarrassed to be incapacitated, ordered him to stand down. "You and I can deal with whatever the hell's going on," he said as he resisted offers of a hand and eventually got to his feet. He prepared to confront the apparition, but it was no longer in the room, which was a relief to the sergeant.

Both were unnerved, and after a few minutes of cursory glances into the downstairs rooms accompanied by halfhearted shouts of "Police!", they wrapped things up. Their report would note that the grounds needed to be cleaned up, and the house should be condemned and razed, but there was no indication of drug use or trespassers.

They omitted the part about the ghostly figure that had

accosted the sergeant, because the shaken officers chose not to include statements that would cause them more work and certain ridicule from their compadres. Nor did they investigate the mysterious lights in the upstairs windows, because they never got past the first floor.

The suggestions about the house and grounds would be passed on to the appropriate city department, where they would go on a long list for eventual disposition. Meanwhile, almost every night the spectral lights continued to move slowly across the windows inside Tartarus House.

CHAPTER SIX

Earlier, senior investigative reporter Jack Blair had walked the few blocks from Channel Nine over to Tartarus House after hearing on the police scanner that cops went there to check things out. He paused on the sidewalk, noting the "KEEP OUT" sign, the broken gate hanging askew, and the foliage, an assortment of dark, twisted plants that bore leaves with unnatural hues—deep purples, blood reds and sickly greens. Strange mushrooms sprouted from the damp soil as wisps of ethereal fog drifted through the yard, carried by a sudden breeze that wasn't there earlier.

"How have I not noticed this place before?" he mused aloud as he entered "Tartarus House" into Google on his phone. Abner McJunkin popped up first, the Union general who had occupied the house after the city fell in the Battle of New Orleans on April 25, 1862. One post mentioned it having been an orphanage, and he saw a brief article about a wealthy planter named Bezaliel Moros who built the house in the seventeen hundreds and whose family members lived there for decades. One of a handful of

French Quarter buildings that survived the devastating fire of 1788, it had been many things since. Today it was a crumbling, abandoned residence.

The house was in terrible shape and appeared unfit for habitation, but Jack knew people were inside—cops for sure, but perhaps others. From its open front door came shouts, and beams of light played over the cracked windowpanes. The investigator in him became curious, so he trespassed just like Angie Bovida had done.

As he picked his way through the thick, gnarly weeds, he heard muffled shouts from inside. Someone yelled the word "police" twice. Seconds later, two uniformed officers emerged onto the porch, came down the rickety stairs, and confronted Jack.

The man in charge, a sergeant, said, "Who are you, and what are you doing here?"

"I'm Jack Blair with Channel Nine. What happened in there?"

The cop pointed to Jack's cellphone. "Turn that off."

"Why? I'm not doing anything wrong."

"You're trespassing on private property. Now get out of here."

"Seriously, Sergeant? Aren't we all trespassing? Do you have a warrant? I doubt it. Help me out. What's going on here?"

"Some strange shit, that's for sure. Put your phone away. Don't quote me, and I'll tell you what happened to us."

Jack agreed, and the cop told him why they'd come and what they'd found. He included seeing a mysterious figure—a woman, or so it seemed to him—but conveniently omitted the part about his collapsing on the floor.

"What's your take on it?" Jack asked.

The burly cop shrugged. "Haven't got a clue. Never encountered something like that before. It's like a show on

Netflix, you know?" He motioned to the other cop, and they walked to the sidewalk, leaving Jack standing a few steps from the rickety porch and the yawning darkness that lay beyond the front door.

What the hell, I'm already here. If there's a woman inside, the worst she can do is run me off. He climbed the ancient stairs, avoided rotten places as he crossed the porch, switched on his phone recorder, and gave two quick raps on the doorframe.

"Hello? Anybody home?"

From somewhere deep inside, there arose a tinkling noise, a cross between a child's laughter and the sound of tiny bells. He stepped inside the front room, and the sound stopped. Now the only sound was the creak of floorboards as he ventured further into the dusty parlor. A whisper echoed through the house—words, perhaps, but too faint to understand—and an icy chill filled the air.

Alarmed but determined to unravel this mystery, Jack brushed off a shiver and crossed into the dining room, where the sergeant had encountered what he called a witch. Seeing no one, he turned and walked down a narrow, dark hallway, using the light from his phone to find his way. Passing a door, he tried the knob, but found it locked. He came to another, rattled the knob, and kept walking. But then there came a sound—a muffled thump—and he turned back.

Is there something behind that door? He rapped two times, then leaned in to listen. There came two quick knocks in response, followed by faint words.

"Help me! Whoever's out there, help me!"

Jack twisted the doorknob in both directions, but he'd need a skeleton key to open the ancient lock. "Hang on a minute! I'm going to help you," he shouted before running down the hallway into a nineteen twenties-era kitchen. As he pulled out drawers, looking for the junk drawer everyone had, he found tarnished silverware, knives and utensils, pencils and pads of paper, and at last, the drawer of odds and ends, including a bag filled with assorted keys, including several old-fashioned skeleton keys that were exactly what he was looking for.

He tried several before the knob turned with a distinctive click. Jack pulled open the door and found a female standing there, covered head to toe in grimy dirt and cobwebs. She rushed out and grabbed him. "Thank God! Get us out of here before he comes back!"

Who are you talking about? he wanted to ask, but she was frantic. Knowing there would be time for answers later, Jack led her down the hallway and across the front room to the door. She rushed outside, crossed the porch, and stumbled into the yard, cursing as she maneuvered through the tangled undergrowth. As he walked through the open door, Jack heard the tinkly sound again—a cross between laughter and childish words. But this time he understood them.

Come back and play with us!

CHAPTER SEVEN

The woman Jack had rescued fell once, then again as she ran recklessly through the tangled, gnarly undergrowth in the front yard. He followed as she rushed through the gate, ran half a block, and turned into St. Ann Street. As she crossed Bourbon, panting furiously, he caught up when she stopped for a breath.

"Thanks for saving my life."

"Who are you? How'd you get in there? What on earth happened to you?"

"I'm Angie Bovida. I'm from Mississippi, and I went there because I'm interested in haunted houses. Come on, get me away from here, and I'll tell you everything you want to know."

"My office is three blocks away. We can talk there." He took her arm and calmed her as they walked. When they reached the destination on Royal Street, she looked up at the sign hanging above the doorway: WCCY-TV, The Voice of the Crescent City. She jerked her arm out of his grasp and stepped away.

"Why are you bringing me to a TV station?" She was furious, and he realized she thought he intended to capitalize on her plight. "Let me explain, please. I'm Jack Blair; I work here. I'm an investigative reporter, and a lot of it deals with the paranormal. I went to that house after the police were dispatched to check out strange things going on. Come in, we'll go to my office, and I'll get you something to eat and drink, and we can call the police if you want."

Calm for the first time, she patted his arm and smiled. "Forgive me, Jack Blair. I recognize you now. We get Channel Nine over in Gulfport, and I've seen you on TV. What better person than you to tell my story to? No cops, at least for now. Get me a donut and a cup of coffee, and I'll tell you everything I know about what happened."

Locked in a tiny room, Angie hadn't heard about the Harbingers. Jack explained what had happened, adding that was why he'd gone to Tartarus House—to find out if another mysterious event might be happening in the old mansion.

Angie took half an hour to freshen up and place a call to her mother, who surprised Angie by saying she was staying in a nearby hotel. She rushed to the TV studio, and after a tearful reunion, Mrs. Bovida sat in the shadows, watching as a director and cameraman prepared for Angie's interview. When everything was set, the director paged Jack, who walked into the studio with Landry Drake. Asking forgiveness for calling the famous paranormal investigator without their advance permission, Jack learned that Mrs. Bovida had gone to Landry for help, only to be told she should go to the police instead. Despite his rebuff, she was grateful he had come today. Angie was as well, and said she hoped Landry's insight might help them understand what was going on inside Tartarus House.

The relationship between Jack and Landry went back several years. They'd met when Jack was living in a box across the street from the haunted Toulouse Street building now occupied by Landry's Paranormal Network. Landry had worked for Channel Nine, and after getting to know Jack, he saw potential in the homeless alcoholic, gave him a job, and celebrated his victories as he became a successful investigator. When Landry left the station to create his new network, he helped Jack get his position as senior investigative reporter. Although Channel Nine no longer created its own supernatural programming since Landry's departure, Jack investigated every paranormal event he heard about. He remained good friends with Cate, Henri, and Landry, and they often called on him for extracurricular help. He loved digging into mysterious and unexplained phenomena as much as they, which explained why he'd spent the last few days running here and there in the French Quarter as the Harbingers began.

Today in the studio, Landry chatted with his former co-workers before the filming started. When the director announced it was time, he took a chair next to Mrs. Bovida while Angie settled in before a video camera, coffee at hand as the director counted down from five to one, dropped his arm, and the interview began.

Angie told her story, explaining why she went to Dauphine Street—the notation in a guidebook that called Tartarus House "a genuinely frightening place" and the eyewitness account of a Civil War general that captured her imagination. "I'm interested in this kind of stuff," she said to Jack. "How scary could it be?"

She told herself it was just an old house, but once she stood outside the fence and saw the ancient mansion looming past a tangled mess of weeds and vines and plaster statues standing sentinel behind gnarly bushes, a wave of fear swept over her. The house had an aura of eerie malevolence that gave her chills.

Mustering up the courage to finish what she'd begun, Angie pushed through the weeds, crossed the porch, and found the door unlocked. "Hello?" she'd shouted, and the only response was a deep, drawn-out moan that echoed in the rooms. "That's just the house settling," she assured her unbelieving self.

Careful with every step she took in the half-light, she entered a room caught in a time warp—peeling wallpaper, dusty portraits hanging askew, ruined chairs and tables, an ancient RCA console radio, and a massive Oriental rug that must have cost a fortune. Now it lay in tattered strips, ravaged by moths and neglected for decades.

She crossed into another room, this one a dining room with a once-magnificent crystal chandelier that now lay in pieces atop a long table. It was then that she heard a noise—a sound like tiny bells, followed by a quiet laugh.

"Who's there?" she recalled crying out as the air grew thick with a suffocating malevolence. Angie found it hard to draw a breath, as if something was gripping her throat. She turned to flee, but blocking the doorway behind her hovered a menacing figure wearing a long, black robe, its face shrouded by a loose cowl.

Angie shrieked, gasped for breath, and collapsed onto the floor. "I guess I fainted," she said, explaining how she awoke in a closet that had a reinforced door frame and batting on every wall that would have silenced noise. The cell—for that was unmistakably its purpose—contained a simple cot and a bucket. It was custom-made for solitary confinement.

She had no way of knowing how long she had been locked in the tiny room, she didn't wear a watch, and she'd lost her phone somewhere in the house. As the minutes ticked away, Angie's heart pounded in her chest. *I'm going to die!* she thought more than once before grim determination set in. If she was to die, let it be while trying to escape, not while sitting in a cell awaiting her fate. She stood and with trembling hands felt along the rough walls, desperate for any sign of a hidden passage. When her fingertips brushed over layers of cobwebs and dust, she recoiled but pressed on, fueled by a desire to escape the clutches of the mysterious thing that had kidnapped her.

Angie stopped talking and asked Jack if she could have a moment to settle her nerves. The next part of her tale had terrified her, and she needed to calm herself before relating it. Jack called for a ten-minute break, after which everyone took their places and the interview resumed.

Trapped in the dark room, she felt it grow increasingly colder. As her feelings of dread intensified, she whispered, "There's no way for the wind to blow in here," and wondered if she was alone. Moving faster, she worked her way along the walls, and she stumbled as her shoe caught on a loose floorboard. With a surge of hope, she knelt and pried until it cracked open. Suppressing her revulsion, she inserted first her hand, then her entire arm into the void, and she learned there was a crawlspace beneath the floor perhaps two feet in height. It would be tight, but God willing, there would be enough room for her to make her escape.

Angie removed a second board, then one more, and suppressing a numbing wave of revulsion, she mustered the courage to squeeze her body into the cramped, cobweb-laden darkness. Driven by her determination to escape, she had entered a recess beneath the floor that would become her coffin if there was no exit. Once she moved away from the hole she'd crept through, she doubted she could ever return, because shuffling her body forward was easy, but doing it backward would have been impossible. *Someday they'll find my body down here under the floor,* she worried as she inched forward on her belly.

Her heart pounded in her ears, drowning out the muffled sound of her own breathing as the crawlspace became a winding labyrinth. She continued, squeezing her way through the cramped space like a slithering snake, and saw a faint glimmer of light piercing a crack in the floorboards just ahead. She moved to it, breathing a little easier as the crawlspace gradually widened until she lay under the light.

With all her might, Angie pushed the boards that formed the crawlspace's ceiling, trying each board until one split with a resounding crack. She redoubled her efforts, and soon she had created a space large enough to shimmy through. She emerged into an empty room, faint rays of light filtering through a grimy window.

In the Channel Nine studio, Angie smiled at Jack and said, "That's when you knocked on the door. Thank God you came. I thought I was going to die in that house!"

"Earlier you described seeing someone in a dark cowl," Jack said. "When I found you, you said you had to get away from him. Did you get a look at his face?"

She paused a moment. "I don't recall. I must have passed out from fright. The person, or thing, or whatever— it was tall, and it wore a cowl that shrouded its face in darkness."

"You heard tinkly voices when you entered the house," Jack continued. "I heard them too when you and I left— light, whispery voices that asked if we could play with them."

"Those are ghosts," Angie said as a shiver ran down her spine. "I'm sure there are ghosts in that house."

As the interview wrapped, Jack extended his gratitude to her for agreeing to do it. He emphasized how significant her revelations had been, and she was excited to tell people back home she was going to be on a television show.

He closed by saying that the haunted houses of the French Quarter had always fascinated him. Countless stories of otherworldly encounters were sometimes the stuff of folklore or alcohol-fueled experiences, but other tales were verifiable and true. People with no reason to lie reported spine-tingling, terrifying experiences in certain venues, and those were corroborated time and again by others.

Tartarus House had long been reputed to be one of the

city's most haunted mansions, and now an eyewitness claimed it was true. Jack had felt and heard things too, and as the taping ended, he couldn't have known how much the spooky house on Dauphine Street would affect his life and the lives of his friends.

CHAPTER EIGHT

Amid a whirlwind of unexplainable occurrences, a very odd thing happened to Landry and Cate. On the same Friday night as the bizarre Mardi Gras parade incident downtown, they went to the Bombay Club to hear a famous clarinet player. It was close to midnight when they walked home down Royal Street. As they turned on St. Philip and approached their building, they noticed something in the shadows at the entryway. It was small, and it had a tail that began wagging furiously as they approached.

There sat a puppy, bright-eyed, long-legged and so skinny his bones showed. The dog yawned and stretched when they approached. "Are you lost, little guy?" Cate asked, bending down to pat the brown pup, whose tail wagged even faster as he rested his head on her knee.

"More likely somebody dumped him," Landry said. "Maybe someone will come along and take him home."

Cate didn't think so. Their quiet, residential street got far less foot traffic than the ones that intersected it on both ends. In the growing darkness, no one would see a small dog sitting on their stoop. "Let's take him upstairs and let him spend the night. I can feed him, and tomorrow we'll decide what to do with him."

"The last thing we need is a dog."

"I'm not saying keep him. It's too late to take him to the SPCA, and I don't want him to sit out here all alone in the dark."

Landry wasn't buying it. "I'll bet he's spent a lot of time by himself in the dark. He's a stray, Cate. A puppy somebody didn't want. We don't have time to mess with a dog."

"Just for tonight." She smiled, and as she picked him up, he put his muzzle against her neck and gave her a warm lick. "He likes me."

"You're probably getting all his fleas and ticks. I'm going to have to hose you down."

"Come on, Grinch. Who knows? You may end up liking him too. Right, Simba?"

"Simba? What makes you think that's his name?"

"It's his name now. He's a brave boy, and he needs a strong, brave name."

"We're not keeping him, Cate. Period."

She flashed a big smile and carried Simba up the stairs, whispering in his floppy ear, "We'll see about that, won't we?"

Landry knew he had a battle ahead of him. They'd talked often about how many dogs had been in the Adams household in Galveston during Cate's childhood. There were always two around, sometimes three, and they were house dogs. One, a tricolor beagle she named Lexie, had been her dog. She picked her out at the kennel, and Lexie had slept under the covers in Cate's bed every night. When she grew old and had to be euthanized, Cate had cried for days.

Landry's childhood in Jeanerette, Louisiana, was nothing like Cate's. There had been outside dogs now and then, but never in the house. Dogs were for hunting or tracking, but not for snuggling and playing with. If one got run over or wandered off, no one shed a tear. Landry didn't have the canine connection Cate did, but he gave this little puppy one thing—he was a really cute boy—bright-eyed, frisky and intelligent.

Cate put an old blanket on the bathroom floor for the little dog to sleep on, and as if he knew what was expected, he sniffed the covers, turned around three times, lay down, and stretched his front and back legs out as far as he could. Then he closed his eyes.

"He seems comfortable here," Cate said, and Landry reminded her something had to be done with him tomorrow. That brought another smile.

CHAPTER NINE

Landry awoke the next morning to find Cate's side of the bed empty. He padded into the kitchen, noticed she'd made a pot of coffee, and looked around the apartment, but she wasn't there. Neither was the dog. He poured a cup and sat at a table on the balcony off their bedroom. A few minutes later she called to him from the street below.

"Landry, look down here! Simba and I have been out for a walk!" The brown dog trotted along St. Philip Street beside her, clearly enjoying the outing, and Landry wondered where Cate had gotten a leash and collar. When she and the stray he refused to call by the name she'd given him reached the third floor, he asked her what was up with that.

"I got up early and walked over to Walgreens on Royal Street. He needed food, and they also had collars and leashes. He ate like a horse, by the way. I don't think he's had a square meal in a while."

I'm sure he hasn't, Landry thought. *Or a bath, or worm medicine, or flea and tick spray. But despite all that, he spent last night in our bathroom.*

Landry's phone chimed with a call from Henri

Duchamp, the third partner in the Paranormal Network, asking if they had time to drop by the office to see something interesting. Landry said they'd be there within the hour, Henri rarely asked them to come in on weekends, and with the supernatural activity going on all over the French Quarter, he thought perhaps there was news to report.

With no place to leave him, Landry agreed Cate could bring the little mutt. Simba handled the leash well, keeping close to Cate's leg and away from people and other dogs as they walked down Chartres a few blocks to the haunted building on Toulouse Street that housed both their studio and Henri's Louisiana Society for the Paranormal.

When they arrived, they found a line of people standing on the sidewalk outside their entryway. Landry looked away, but people recognized him and yelled, "There he is! Landry, talk to us, please! What are the Harbingers all about?"

"No time," he muttered as Cate unlocked the front gate that led both to a ground-floor restaurant and the stairway up to their offices and studio. She secured it behind them, and they walked down the carriageway to the stairs. Despite the small but clamorous assemblage outside, everything indoors was quiet this morning, a pleasant, striking contrast to the mob who had clambered up these stairs yesterday in hopes of meeting Landry.

The second floor was their office area, open in the middle and with cubicles around the perimeter. There they found Henri and a man sporting a plaid golf cap in the conference room, poring over an ancient set of floor plans that lay spread on the table.

Henri waved them in. "Landry! Cate! Come and meet my friend Jules Beckman. I'm remiss in not introducing you long before this; over the years, Jules has helped me many times; and this morning I find myself on the receiving end once again! You may recall Jules is the curator of the Louisiana State Museum at the Cabildo. But he's far more than that!" He paused and gave his friend a wink. "As the saying goes, he knows where the bodies are buried. You've been with the museum for how long—forty years?"

"Forty years this fall," the man affirmed. "And don't listen to Henri's mad ravings. There are no bodies buried in the Cabildo—or perhaps I should say I've never come across any!"

The ancient building, the site of the Louisiana Purchase transfer in 1803, stood on Jackson Square next to St. Louis Cathedral. Rebuilt after the destructive Great Fire of 1788, another devastating fire two hundred years later heavily damaged it once again. Although many records had been lost in 1988, more than half had escaped destruction, some dating as far back as the city's founding in 1718.

"Come see what Jules brought us," Henri gushed. "He came upon a treasure trove of floor plans for structures all over *La Nouvelle-Orléans*—the original city that's the French Quarter today. These are the original drawings of my buildings. This is fabulous!"

Henri owned adjoining buildings on Toulouse Street. His nonprofit, the Louisiana Society for the Paranormal, occupied the one next door, where its three floors held offices, archives, and an extensive library of literature dealing with the supernatural and unexplained. He'd bought the building where they stood today as an investment, renting the upper floors to the new Paranormal Network he, Landry and Cate formed. A bar and restaurant called Cajun Pride Brewery occupied the ground floor, and stairs off the carriageway led to their offices on the second floor and a production studio on the third.

This was a haunted building, something all of them had experienced firsthand when Landry had unraveled a murder mystery from the eighteenth century and discovered that the paranormal phenomenon called age regression was real.

That mystifying case became an episode called "Die Again" on Landry's popular television series *The Bayou Hauntings*.

The building creaked and groaned so often that those sounds were ignored, but other phenomena gave them goosebumps. They would arrive at work to find furniture rearranged. They often heard footsteps on the stairways and mournful cries from the third floor, where hapless indentured people had been chained long ago. Sometimes they felt bursts of cold air and caught the scent of lilac perfume lingering in the room that had been Prosperine LaPiere's boudoir when she and Lucas lived on the second floor in the early 1800s.

Pieces of the fragile drawing flaked away as Jules smoothed the pages and pointed to faded lines and words. "The past two hundred years haven't been kind to these old sheets," he commented, a hint of sadness in his voice. As with Henri, his passion for historical artifacts was a part of his psyche.

The two were history buffs, but different in most other ways. Unlike his bachelor friend Henri, Jules was a widower who enjoyed a good meal and fine wine, although his state paycheck afforded him less opportunity to indulge than Henri. Jules lived not in a fine Garden District mansion but a small third-floor walkup off Magazine Street. Working in dusty archives every day, he wore practical clothing, whereas Henri usually sported a three-piece suit, even in the humid dog days of a New Orleans summer.

"Jules came across these fascinating plans in an old box in the Cabildo's basement," Henri gushed. "They're an incredible source of information—an insight into how buildings were designed and constructed in the eighteenth century, back when New Orleans was a new port city."

Jules nodded. "They were a surprising find. Over two hundred years ago, somebody dumped dozens of floor plans into that old crate. It's surprising they survived two major fires. They're all written in French or Spanish, which means they predate the Louisiana Purchase in 1803. I'm hoping to match the old plans to existing structures and turn them over to the owners, as I've done for Henri today. I think they'd be glad to have them."

"Anything exciting so far?" Landry asked, looking at the plans from a bird's-eye view and seeing the rooms laid out just as they were today. A window here and a door there had been added or taken away, but otherwise the thick old walls were the same. Over two centuries, the buildings had faced fires and hurricanes and threats of demolition after standing vacant for decades, yet they survived.

Landry saw something odd on the floor plan, pointed at a spot on the paper, and said, "I don't understand what that is. This is the room we're in right now, correct? So where's that door? And look! There's a room behind it. It looks like it runs between the buildings. Am I reading this correctly?"

Henri smiled. "Well, Jules, it seems he's found our enigma already! Landry, someone plastered over that door a long time ago. It's on that wall"—he pointed across the room—"and I'm going to open it up to see what's there. The contractors would have worked from this drawing provided by Lucas LaPiere, who owned the property. That means he knew it was there. I'm wondering if it's a passageway between the buildings, although I don't think LaPiere owned the other one. Either way, what was its purpose?"

Landry examined the plan and pointed again. "What's that black square near the back wall of the hidden room?"

Jules replied, "I don't know; maybe when Henri gets inside, we'll learn the answer." Jules said the room was about fifteen feet long and ten wide and extended through two sets of brick exterior walls, each three feet thick. At least that was how it appeared on the drawing; the finished room might not have actually extended to the next building.

They would only find out when the room was opened.

Jules asked to see the ownership records Henri had received when he bought the adjoining building. He brought over a thick file from his office, and Jules pored through the earliest pages until he said, "Aha!" as he poked a finger at a yellowed document. "Now this makes a little sense. Lucas owned both buildings after all! LaPiere et Cie bought the land and constructed the building next door. That's Luca's company, and that passage proves both were built at the same time. Speaking of time, I must run. Later today, I'll look through the box of plans to see if there's one for that building too.

"By the way, call me anytime if you need help with research," Jules said to Landry as he walked to the stairs, and Landry asked if a floor plan might exist for the oddly named Tartarus House in the 800 block of Dauphine Street, explaining that he was looking for historical background on one of the oldest houses in the city.

"I know the house," Jules replied. "And you're right; it's reputed to be the oldest dwelling still standing in the Quarter. But Landry, I call bullshit, if you'll pardon my gutter slang." He smiled and continued, "You're not looking for historical background on an old house. That place is seriously haunted, you're a paranormal expert, and that means you're looking for something else.

"As to the floor plan, that old crate is full of papers. Why don't you come to the Cabildo and look through them yourself?" They agreed to a time tomorrow, and after he left, Landry mentioned how helpful Jules might prove to them. Henri agreed, saying the resources at the man's fingertips were of incalculable value. That statement would soon prove true, when Jules uncovered another document hidden away deep in the ancient archives of the Cabildo.

CHAPTER TEN

Just after eight the next morning, long before the Cabildo and the museum opened to the public, Landry and Simba stood in Pirate's Alley before a heavy wooden door with no markings. He texted Jules, and moments later the curator opened the door and told Landry to come in.

Landry hesitated and pointed to the dog. "Apologies for showing up with Simba. I didn't expect to be responsible for him this morning. He's developed a habit of barking for hours if we leave him crated in our apartment. My girlfriend had a doctor's appointment, so he's all mine. Just tell me if he can't come in, and we can do this another time."

Jules smiled. "I've loved dogs all my life. Wish I had one now, but since all I do is work, he'd be alone too much of the time. The moment I retire, I'm heading to the shelter." He knelt and patted the dog. "Simba, if your father keeps you on the leash and you don't make noise or stick your nose where it doesn't belong, we'll get along fine. Come on in, men."

I'm not your father, Landry muttered to Simba as they climbed a broad staircase and entered a cramped, windowless office in the upper reaches of the ancient building. Landry took a seat in the only chair at the only table, thinking how much the tiny space resembled an interrogation room at a police station. As if he understood he'd better be on his best behavior, Simba dutifully sat down beside his master's leg.

Parts of the vast building called the Cabildo dated back to 1795, and at their last meeting Jules had mentioned how difficult it was to find things stored in the warren of dimly lit rooms and dusty hallways. Displays in the Louisiana State Museum on the Cabildo's first floor held only a fraction of the items; dozens of dusty storerooms held thousands more that dated back to the founding of New Orleans.

By now it was too late to create a comprehensive inventory. Over the years, there had been efforts to computerize the hundreds of thousands of artifacts and papers, but the time and expense of such a project were so daunting that less than ten percent had been digitized. It took the memories of longtime employees like Jules Beckman to remember the locations of relics—cannonballs, muskets, swords, armor, bibles and crucifixes that lay on rows of steel shelves and in dusty boxes filled with memorabilia and documents.

Yesterday Landry had asked about a plan for the Tartarus House on Dauphine, and Jules had done some searching. With a grin, he told Landry his efforts had been somewhat successful. He hadn't uncovered a plan, but he had found a good deal of information about the mansion.

"I mentioned earlier it's the oldest house in the Quarter," he said as he hoisted a tattered storage box onto the table. "This stuff relates to early construction in French New Orleans. There's a land deed for that property dated 1722, just a few years after the establishment of the city. It's a miracle the house survived the Great Fire of 1788, which destroyed eighty percent of the French Quarter."

"But you didn't find a floor plan?" Landry asked.

"I haven't discovered one so far, but don't give up hope just yet. I didn't have time to examine the crate in the basement where I found the other plans. I'll leave you to this, and I'll check downstairs later this morning. My office is the third door on the right, so give a shout if you need anything." As he left, Landry leaned down, patted Simba, and said, "You're being a good boy." He licked his master's hand and stretched out on the floor.

Landry removed a stack of papers from the box, the first of which was the land deed Jules had mentioned. *April 7, 1722. A land transfer from the French governor, Jean-Baptiste Le Moyne de Bienville, to one Bezaliel Moros.* Although the document was in French, handwritten with flourishing scrolls and loops, Landry understood the words *Rue Dauphin.* Like many streets in the French Quarter, other than being anglicized to Dauphine Street, the name hadn't changed in three centuries.

He stared at the unusual name. *Bezaliel Moros, like the Krewe of Moros float that mysteriously appeared in a parade the other night. What was it—Greek, perhaps? Or Corsican? What was the connection to the Harbingers?* He made a mental note to find out more.

He sorted through other papers—easements, tax receipts and the like—but there were no more deeds. Making a mental note to learn who owned the property today, he dug deeper and came across a yellowed set of folded pages. He peeled away the top sheet, doing as little damage as possible to the brittle parchment, and saw faded lines that might show this was a floor plan. Was it for the house? He'd have to open the fragile document to find out. Which meant calling Jules, since it wasn't his document to tamper with.

Landry discovered that unfolding a three-hundred-year-old set of papers wasn't as simple as it sounded. After removing as much dust and dirt as possible, Jules put the documents in a humidification chamber and told Landry to come back in four hours. The timing was good because Simba was restless and needed a break. Landry took the dog out to Jackson Square, where he let him do his business and play for a while. After that, he'd have gone to the office, but Simba was persona non grata there today.

This morning in the Paranormal Network's third-floor studio, his crew was filming background footage for an upcoming documentary on phantom ships in the Gulf of Mexico. The studio was soundproofed, but the director insisted that Simba be off premises when they were filming. The young, exuberant dog barked furiously at anything he saw or heard—a spider on the wall, a car door slamming on the street below, or absolutely nothing.

Since he couldn't go to the office, Landry walked a few blocks to check out Tartarus House for the first time. As he turned the corner onto Dauphine Street, a strange sense of foreboding washed over him. He wondered how the weather on the walk over could be warm and humid, while here the air grew heavy, and the sky turned dark and oppressive.

Something was off about this block, as though an invisible weight pressed down on it from above. There was an oppressive, mournful feeling of dread, and he wasn't the only one to notice it. The dog whimpered softly and moved close to his master. He shivered and gave a yelp, and Landry said, "Hey, buddy. Let's just walk past the house and get this over with. This place gives me the creeps. You too, I see."

The mansion stood tall and imposing, its weathered facade bearing the marks of time. Ivy crawled up its sides, and the weed-infested front yard bore witness no one seemed to care about it any longer. Landry approached the gate and saw the name *Tartarus House* on the weathered sign, but that was far enough for Simba. He refused to go a step further, pulling hard on his leash and barking in short, scared yips.

"What is it, boy? Come on. Let's at least go into the yard. There's nothing to be afraid of." But the dog resisted, doing his best to move Landry away. He had read about dogs having extrasensory capabilities, and this old house spooked Simba so badly that he would have no part of going inside that fence. Frankly, Landry had reservations too. Things really were off, it had been a beautiful morning when they left the Cabildo, but now ominous clouds filled the sky, and thunder rolled as if burdened by the weight of the secrets that existed on the grounds and within the weathered walls of the ancient mansion where they stood.

They left, and Simba picked up his gait a block off Dauphine, where the sky again became bright and cloudless. The sudden weather changes puzzled Landry, and he wondered if this was part of the Harbingers. So far no one knew why they were happening. Perhaps the phenomenon on Dauphine Street was part of the mystery.

Cate texted to say she was at the apartment and could take Simba, so Landry ran by to drop him off before returning to the Cabildo, which he found teeming with visitors. Landry pushed his way through the crowd and climbed the stairs to an area on the top floor restricted to staff only, where Jules met him at a checkpoint and escorted him to his office.

"I think this document is the one you wanted," Jules said, gesturing at the floor plan lying on a table. Although all the notations were in French, Landry noticed a block in the upper right corner that contained words in a flowery script. He saw a date and a name, the same one he'd observed on the 1722 land grant.

Tartarus House. Bezaliel Moros, Owner. May 1723.

"I'd like your opinion about the name Moros," Landry said. "I hadn't heard it until that phantom float for the nonexistent Krewe of Moros. That can't be a coincidence. I looked it up; it's a Greek surname but also a god who can predict doom. Do you believe there's some connection to the Harbingers?"

Jules replied, "I've done extensive research on Bezaliel Moros. Let's have a look at this document, and then I'll tell you what I've learned." He said the yellowed, brittle paper was the original architectural drawing for Tartarus House, which would become the home of an indigo planter named Moros.

"I'm not sure that reference to his having been an indigo planter is correct," Jules commented. "The Cabildo has extensive records of plantation owners in Louisiana, and his name doesn't appear anywhere. Wherever he came from, he was a man of means, because a mansion this large would cost a fortune."

Landry bent over the fragile paper, looking at the rooms on the first and second floors and their descriptions. The top floor was one enormous room eighty by sixty feet in size, with smaller rooms at either end. He asked Jules if it was meant to be a ballroom.

"Without a doubt; it's typical for grand houses of the time. Also probably rarely used, but from my research over the years, I've learned that every self-respecting, successful mansion owner had to have one. It was a sort of status symbol. You didn't have to host many fancy balls; you just had to have a room big enough to prove you could."

Landry pointed to the plan. "The smaller rooms that lie at either end of the ballroom—are they for storage? And take a look at that." He pointed to a black square that lay in one of the rooms. "The same square is on the floor plan of Henri's building. In the hidden room."

"You're correct. The black squares are interesting. Perhaps it's a stretch, but I wonder if they represent the same thing, or perhaps they're connected in some way."

"Connected? Literally?"

Jules grinned. "That would be a stretch, wouldn't it? Some kind of supernatural passageway between two places? That's your bailiwick, not mine. No, I'm thinking they might have been built for the same purpose, whatever that might be. Maybe someday we'll learn more if Henri decides to look for his secret room."

Switching subjects, Landry said, "I went by the house after I left you earlier. It's a spooky place, and it looks like it's been abandoned for decades. I had the dog with me, and he got so scared he wouldn't let me look around. The weather even turned gloomy on that block. I'm going back to see if I can get inside. Can you make me a copy of this drawing?"

"I'll make you a copy, but again I'll caution you that it's one of the city's most haunted houses. Some people claim there have been more supernatural events there than anywhere else in the city. You'd know more about that than I. I'm just saying be careful, Landry. I wouldn't go inside alone."

"Thanks for the warning, but you're preaching to the choir. I deal in this kind of stuff for a living, you know."

Jules shook his head, wondering how a man with so much knowledge of the paranormal could dismiss the reality of it so lightly. He decided to tell Landry everything he knew about the Moros family and Tartarus House before he let the ghost hunter go wandering off. The information might not deter him, but it could make him more vigilant.

CHAPTER ELEVEN

Jules asked Landry to sit for a moment and said, "I know you've gained vast experience in the paranormal field over the past few years, and you're far more an expert than I am. But everything I've learned about this house and this family sends up danger signals. You must be careful going there, and I'd advise against trying to get in. You don't know what might be inside."

"Have you seen it lately? It's a total wreck. Despite Angie Bovida's kidnapping by someone who was there, nobody could live in that house."

"You're the expert. Think outside the box. I'm not talking about someone living there. Bezaliel Moros built the house three hundred years ago. As I mentioned, I don't think he was a planter; that name doesn't come up at all before the governor granted him the land in 1722. How did he get to New Orleans? The names are Greek, but I don't think that many Greeks immigrated to the southern United States in those days.

"Another enigmatic thing is that the title to the house has never changed. The man who built it in 1723 owns it today. Lots of old houses in this town have remained in the same family for generations, but unless they're owned by trusts that exist in perpetuity, they're transferred when an owner dies. If the title remained with a dead person, the heir would receive no benefits—he couldn't get a mortgage or set up the utilities or even legally take possession.

"Back to his odd name. According to Greek mythology, Bezaliel was the god of shadows. His name also means 'damaged' in Greek. He was one of the fallen angels described in the apocryphal book of Enoch."

Landry laughed. "No wonder I haven't heard of him. I don't recall being offered Greek mythology classes in high school or community college."

"I doubt you'd have heard of Bezaliel even if you had. He's a relatively minor god, and his name is rarely mentioned. And how about the unusual last name—Moros."

"Like the Krewe of Moros with the phantom float the other night. What are you getting at?"

"More mythology. Moros is the Greek god of doom. He's been known to appear dressed as a sorcerer or magician. I don't know who the Moros family is or was, or how they got to New Orleans, but in my opinion, it's no coincidence they use these names. That's why I cautioned you, Landry. The supernatural exists in New Orleans, we both know it, and we must be very careful not to step too far from one realm into another."

"Why, Jules, I'm beginning to think you believe in this stuff just like I do."

"I couldn't have worked in the archives at the Cabildo for forty years without coming across things I couldn't explain. The city's full of stories—houses and buildings that are genuinely possessed by entities—or something—from another place or time. As you said, you do this for a living. You know more than I, but you noticed how the weather changed when you approached the house. Even your dog sensed something was wrong."

Landry didn't understand where this was going. "So Bezaliel is a Greek god who showed up in New Orleans three hundred years ago. And you think he's still in the house today. A Greek god in an old house in the French Quarter? That's even a stretch for me to believe."

"Although he's named for a god, he may be something else. And there may be more than one. I'm certain he possesses immortality; look at how long he's been around already. Can he be killed? I don't know. Banished? Perhaps. I don't know where he came from, but I think voodoo was what attracted him to our city. Bezaliel was here when the city was only a few years old, and he likely created a lot of the paranormal events that gave New Orleans a reputation for being haunted. All I can say is that Tartarus House has been their base of operations for centuries."

He paused a moment, then added, "I wasn't joking when I said Tartarus House may be the most haunted in town. Do you know what Tartarus is?" Landry shook his head, and Jules continued, "In Greek mythology, it's the deepest pit of the underworld. In the *Iliad*, it's described as being 'as far beneath Hades as heaven is above earth.' It's a place of horrific torment and suffering where souls are judged after death and the wicked receive their just punishment.

"The name says it all; that house is no 'Oaklawn Manor' or 'Whispering Arms.' No sane, normal person would name his home Tartarus. Please, Landry. Please be careful. Neither of us has any idea what may lay behind those walls."

CHAPTER TWELVE

Landry left with a copy of the floor plan tucked under his arm and walked next door to Muriel's where his friend Claude, the restaurant's maître d', ushered him to his favorite table in a quiet corner of the bar. As usual, several people recognized him; they whispered and pointed, but he was grateful no one approached for an autograph. Today he focused on a single purpose—getting inside Tartarus House. He ordered a glass of wine and ate his lunch absently as he ran through ways he might gain access without encountering anyone.

The sun shone brightly over the French Quarter, and a light breeze stirred the air as Landry strolled back to the old mansion. Approaching Dauphine Street, he noticed the sun dim as shadows lengthened, even though it was midday. As before, when he turned onto the block, a chill swept over him, and ominous clouds rolled in from nowhere. The sounds of laughter and music from nearby Bourbon Street faded away, replaced by an air of desolation and sadness that draped this block of Dauphine Street like a shroud.

There's no sun here because it's blocked by those two-story houses on the opposite side of the street, Landry assured himself while knowing something this odd couldn't easily be explained away. He stood at the gate, watching the wind pick up and the trees in the front yard begin to sway in an eerie symphony. As a feeling of unease settled in Landry's chest, he ignored the KEEP OUT sign on the gate and entered the overgrown front yard. Mustering his courage, he maneuvered through tangled vines and thorny bushes, climbed the stairs, sidestepped the rotten boards on the porch, and stood before the decaying front door.

The sensation that he was being watched crept into his brain, and he glanced behind him as he rattled the doorknob, which didn't budge. Briefly considering kicking the door in, he recalled seeing a back entrance on the floor plan. He stumbled around the house through the undergrowth and arrived at a newer door, this one sturdy and solid. He knocked twice before trying the knob, which turned. He pushed, and to his surprise, the door creaked open.

He stepped inside. "Hello? Is anybody here?" Except for the tick-ticking of a clock somewhere, the house was silent.

The cramped, dusty room where he stood was lined with crude wooden cupboards from floor to ceiling, each crammed with exotic—and some erotic—merchandise. Skull ashtrays, bongs, pipes, red dildos bearing devil faces and masks lay on shelves; one, with a thumbtacked sign labeled "potions," contained hundreds of tiny vials. He looked at the labels on a few—love, health, pleasure—and others with ominous labels such as, destruction, confusion, and loss.

One cabinet held an assortment of old, leather-bound books. He squinted to read the faded names on their rotting spines. *Magick of the Ages. Spells to Charm the Unbeliever. A History of Witchcraft. Secrets of Old New Orleans.*

As a believer in the paranormal who dealt with

supernatural occurrences every day, Landry considered stuff like this—love potions, hexes and the like—garbage foisted on gullible people. He shook his head and wondered aloud who'd be crazy enough to spend money on this junk.

There came a whisper, light as air. A child's voice. "You aren't safe here."

"Who is it? Who said that?" Landry shouted, whirling around to see if someone else was there, but he was alone. He walked into the next room and found a converted kitchen with an old sink, table and refrigerator. Today the room served as a storeroom for long black robes and tall pointy hats with stars on them. No one there either.

There came another sound—the muffled, high-toned twitter of a child laughing—from somewhere in the house. "Who's there?" he yelled as he looked around, opening closet doors filled with dusty boxes, papers and file folders and peering into rooms stacked floor to ceiling with everything from Mardi Gras parade paraphernalia to an antique bicycle and a grotesque, bald female mannequin wearing garish red lipstick and a scarlet robe. A few doors were locked along the central hallway that ran from front to back, splitting the first floor in two. After listening to Angie's interview at Channel Nine, Landry wondered which one of these had been her prison.

The house appeared empty, but the whisper and the laughter had been real. He wasn't the only one here.

Landry looked around, moving through a dining room into a high-ceilinged front parlor with a massive fireplace at one end and rotting furniture strewn about. He cocked his head as the temperature plunged, and the pungent rotten-egg aroma of sulphur filled the room. This wasn't the first time he'd smelled the rank odor, and as a paranormal investigator, he knew what it represented. According to legend, sulphur was the devil's stench—a foul, fetid odor that arose from Hell itself. A rustle came from behind him, and someone spoke.

"What do you think you're doing?"

"Shit!" he yelled, turning to see a man standing in the doorway through which he'd just passed. "Who the hell are you?"

The towering figure had the whitest skin Landry had ever seen. His long blond hair cascaded across his shoulders and down the black robe he wore. He held a tapered baton and projected an aura of power that overwhelmed Landry with a deep sense of uneasiness. *Be careful,* he told himself.

"My name is Proteus Moros, Mr. Drake, and you're trespassing in my house."

Moros? "Uh, I'm sorry. How do you know my name?"

"I know many things. What do you want?"

"I thought the house was unoccupied. I'm sure you'd agree it looks rather…well, never mind. A woman claims to have been kidnapped inside this house by a female wearing a long robe—one like yours, as a matter of fact. I'm here to find out what's going on."

The man seemed amused. "Nothing is *going on*. No one was kidnapped. It's obvious the woman isn't telling the truth."

"But she is. My friend rescued her from a locked room inside this house. Where is she…"

Moros interrupted, his words harsh. "You're confused, Mr. Drake, and you've come to the wrong place. Listen to me; no one has been here—no kidnapper, no trapped woman, no rescuer. Get out. Now."

"That's not right; someone *is* in this house. A moment ago I heard a child's giggly voice saying I wasn't safe here. Where is she?"

His lips curled into a sneer. "You and I are the only living things in this house. Soon it will be just me because you *will leave now.*" The robed man pointed his baton at the locked front door, which flew open. He waited with his arms crossed until Landry walked out, turning to confront the man again. Instead, the door slammed shut, leaving him standing alone on the porch.

Moros. He introduced himself as Proteus Moros. And he said it was his house.

Who the hell is he? How does he know who I am, and what's going on in there? It looks deserted, but why are all those potions and paraphernalia stored in the back rooms?

Angry and frustrated, Landry refused to admit defeat so easily. He gripped the doorknob and turned it, but it was locked once again. Boiling over with rage, he pounded the ancient door with his fist, sending a resounding rattle through it. It was a fleeting, desperate attempt to gain entry to a place he shouldn't be, and he reconsidered the wisdom of such an assault on Proteus Moros's property.

It's foolhardy to challenge him in his own house. I'm likely to get a ride to the police station and publicity I don't need.

He reluctantly accepted retreat as his best option; this was not the time to escalate the situation; this complex mystery had to wait for another day. Calming the emotions swirling within him, Landry gathered his thoughts as he left the gloom of Dauphine Street and rejoined the real world, where the sun in a cloudless sky brought warmth and light to the sidewalks where he walked.

I'll tell the others what happened and get their advice, he thought as he solidified his resolve to go back to Tartarus House, uncover the truth, and unearth whatever secrets lay within its walls. He felt a renewed sense of purpose, and by the time he arrived at the office on Toulouse Street, he was ready to face the challenges ahead and consult with his friends on how best to proceed.

As Henri joined him in the conference room, he called Cate at home on speakerphone and related everything about his two trips to Dauphine Street. He described how Simba got spooked and about encountering the strange man who called himself Proteus Moros. "Jules Beckman told me about Bezaliel Moros but not this guy Proteus. He's obviously a relative, and I wonder if he's the present owner. He rather rudely kicked me out after I…sort of let myself in, I guess you'd say. I didn't believe anyone was in the house. Now that I've been inside, I'm determined to find out what's going on in there."

Cate wasn't having it. "Here you go again, Landry, doing something without thinking it through. What can you accomplish by going back? You saw a man in a black robe standing in his own house. It's Mardi Gras, for God's sake. Everyone's wearing costumes. He ordered you to leave. So what? You broke into his house; you were a trespasser. He had every right to kick you out, and he'll probably call the cops if you show up again causing trouble. If you end up in jail, don't call me to bail you out. If you're that foolhardy, you can deal with the consequences on your own."

"I love you when you're angry," Landry quipped, attempting to save face in front of Henri.

There was an audible click as Cate disconnected.

Their fight that evening—or major disagreement, if one disliked using the word *fight* when describing a domestic dispute—ranked as one of the worst they'd had. Landry thought Cate couldn't accept his need to uncover the secrets of Tartarus House. Cate believed Landry should see a psychiatrist. While trespassing in an old house, he'd confronted the owner about Angie Bovida's supposed kidnapping. Told to leave, he'd continued to badger the man until he forced Landry out. All of that, and he was insisting on going back.

"Cra-zee," she called him more than once, fueling the fires of his irritation.

At last, with no one budging and no cessation of hostilities, they agreed to let things lie for the night.

I wonder sometimes why I put up with this, she thought to herself as she turned her back to him in bed, flipped off the reading lamp, and patted Simba's head.

CHAPTER THIRTEEN

I'm walking down a street in the darkness in surroundings that are comfortably familiar because this is St. Philip, the street where I live. As I cross Bourbon, a group of rowdy boys passes, paying me no attention as they stumble along, their Pat O'Brien's to-go cups filled with potent Hurricanes. "That's Landry Drake, the TV guy," someone shouts, but I move on without acknowledging them.

A light rain begins to fall as I turn on Dauphine Street and approach the old mansion that stands in the next block. Ghostly shadows dance and sway as wisps of moonlight, eerily visible through the broken clouds, play upon its weathered, crumbling walls. Its windows, broken and jagged, stare at me like empty eyes.

I stand at the gate as the air grows stagnant and heavy, as though the once-verdant garden is stained with the lingering presence of long-lost souls. What tragic events and unspeakable horrors unfolded within those haunted walls?

Dark windows on the third floor are shadowed by the eaves. Is that a candle flickering as someone holding it moves past the window? Perhaps it is an illusion or the reflection of a moonbeam. Surely no one is inside this crumbling mansion, walking its lonely halls and musty rooms.

Although the thought causes me to tremble, I must walk past the grotesque statues that leer at me from the tangled undergrowth in the garden. The house beckons me; I've been here before, but that was in the daytime. Now it's midnight, and in the darkness, everything about it has become more malevolent and forbidding.

I am aware that this is a dream, and all I must do to avoid harm is awaken. I cross the yard, climb the stairs, and turn the knob. This time the door opens silently into a house where darkness reigns supreme. The scent of decay lingers in every corner, mingling with dampness and mold.

Were these rooms ever filled with life and laughter? Legends and rumors abound of the mansion's tragic past and the restless spirits trapped within these walls, doomed to wander the halls for eternity. Some claim to have seen the ghosts of children drifting aimlessly past the broken windows, moaning for the peace that will forever elude them.

I walk down a dank hallway to a rickety staircase, and I ascend, taking care where I step. The risers creak mightily, and once, when I pause to listen, I hear other sounds— distant whispers punctuated by a faint cry. "Please help me!" Someone may be crying out, although it could be nothing more than the creaks and groans of an old house.

The second floor is unfamiliar to me, and I walk down a long hallway past closed doors on both sides. Looking for access to the ballroom, I open each and glance inside to find bedrooms and parlors furnished with rotting bedsteads, couches, chairs and rugs. Everything carries the stench of age and neglect, and a sense of unease arises within me. This house is not a warm, friendly place. It has never been. Evil things took place here. Men and women died here—children too—in unspeakably horrific ways.

But why? What secrets does this house keep close?

At last I find it—a door that hides a narrow staircase. My shoulders brush against the walls as I go up, dislodging paint and plaster and exposing narrow wooden laths. I reach the top riser and face another closed door. I glance at the tiny space at the bottom of the door, and I see a flicker of light.

Is it the candle I noticed from the street? My heart throbs wildly as I turn the knob and push the door. It opens only a few inches because something is blocking it from the other side. I use my shoulder to push harder, and soon I have created a space I can squeeze through. Inside at last, I shine my light around the cavernous ballroom, and what lies before me is both puzzling and unsettling.

I have studied the floor plan for this house. There is one way to reach the third floor and one way out, and that is the stairway behind me. Anyone in this room must leave by the door I just pushed open, yet…from the inside…someone has stacked cartons and heavy furniture to form a barricade.

Why would a person block the only entrance? How could he accomplish that and get out himself? Unless he used ropes to rappel from the top of the porch down the side of the house, which is unlikely,, it is a physical impossibility. So he must still be here, and the thought frightens me.

I'm limiting my thinking. I'm in a dream, and this is a haunted house. It has been so for centuries. Why does it have to have been a person who blocked the doorway? I sense the other entities present in this drafty old house, things that occupy a realm beyond the scope of logic and understanding. I come to accept that it was one of those entities that barricaded the only entrance to this floor.

Now I am compelled to learn why.

My dream ends; I awaken drenched in sweat even

though our bedroom is cool. Cate breathes softly beside me, and I'm gratified I haven't interrupted her sleep. I lie awake, thinking. I was inside the house on Dauphine Street just yesterday, and the unexpected confrontation with Proteus Moros was unsettling and more than a little scary. That's why I dreamed about the house; it weighs heavily on my mind. Now I must sleep again. I force thoughts of the house from my brain and concentrate on good things— Cate, our new puppy, and the prospect of uncovering a hidden room at the office.

Time passes, and I fall asleep again, only to join the dream where I left it.

———

The door that leads to the third-floor ballroom is blocked once again, and I am on the stairway, trying to open it. Is the person—if it is a person—in the ballroom on the other side of this door? It stands to reason that he must be.

But dreams are unconstrained by logic. I struggle with the door, and like before, I create sufficient space to squeeze through. Moonbeams struggle to penetrate the grimy panes of glass that haven't been cleaned in years. The result is a half-light that casts eerie shadows on the walls and leaves most of the room shrouded in darkness.

What was that noise? Is someone else here? Is it the person—the thing—who barricaded the door? I hold my breath and stand like a statue, listening. The only sounds are the ones I've heard everywhere, the creaks and groans of an ancient mansion dealing with age and neglect.

I hear something else—a hissing, fizzing sound emanating from the dark end of the ballroom. And a quiet scrape, scrape, as though...

...as though something over there in the gloom is crawling toward me.

I am terrified because even though I do not know who

or what my adversary is, I know it intends to kill me. My only thought is of survival. I must escape quickly—I must squeeze back through the door, race down the narrow stairs, and flee this house before I become its next victim.

Now there is another sound, one that is much closer, and as I step back, I trip over a box and fall to the wooden floor. The hissing noise is loud and somehow terrifying. As I stand, wisps of delicate gossamer caress my cheeks, my arms. I brush them away but feel many more that hang like gauzy threads from somewhere above. My efforts to dispel them are fruitless; with every touch, the tiny filaments adhere to my skin and my clothing.

Movement is difficult, as I am constrained by thousands of these gossamer strings. With effort, I shuffle to the door where my path to freedom lies. As I prepare to sidle through, I glance up. A stray moonbeam illuminates the ceiling fifteen feet above me, and I see an enormous...thing. Is it hanging from the chandelier? No, the fixture is too far away. It's huge and black and...oh, my God. The creature feverishly spins more gossamer threads, sending them downward to impede my escape!

My legs become entangled, and I tear at the webbing, wedging my body into the narrow space that leads out. Too late I realize that I can barely move now. I am encircled by the tiny fibers, and I tumble down the cramped staircase. As I fall, the doorway behind me opens wide. The crates and boxes are gone, and now I understand about that thing that's still up there, supported by its filmy web as it waits up near the ceiling. And I know what it wants.

It's waiting for me to stop struggling.

CHAPTER FOURTEEN

Drenched in sweat, Landry awoke, gasping deep breaths as his heart pounded. Cate lay next to him, breathing softly. Somehow he'd managed not to awaken her during either dream, even while battling his way through the most vivid nightmares he'd ever experienced. He tiptoed to the bathroom, retrieved shorts, socks and shoes, and opened the door into the living room. He whispered to Simba, who stretched, yawned, and followed his master. Landry closed the door behind them; there would be no more sleep tonight. It was almost six a.m., and he might as well get the day started. He knew there was someone else who'd like that idea.

Simba wagged his tail and rolled over so Landry could rub his tummy. "Hey, little boy," he said, patting the lanky dog, who responded by licking Landry's hand and squirming with ecstatic wiggles. "Give me a minute, and we'll go for a walk, buddy." He put on his clothes, hooked Simba's leash to his collar, and led the pup downstairs.

"I guess I'm getting used to you, Simba," he said as the dog trotted along beside him. "To be honest, it's kind of nice having you around. But don't tell your mom I said that, okay? We'll let her think you're her dog." The little boy understood none of it, but by Landry's expression and tone of voice, Simba understood that his master was talking to him, and he wagged his tail.

They strolled over to the Moonwalk, a promenade that ran for a mile alongside the Mississippi River. It was a place Landry loved, although he rarely saw it at this hour. As they ran upriver, he saw the Big Easy awakening on a new day. Massive cargo ships passed in silence, workers milled about a construction site as the familiar beep-beep-beep of heavy equipment in reverse signaled the beginning of a shift, and rowdy tourists who'd been up all night crowded into Café du Monde for a beignet and a shot of chicory coffee before turning in.

As he and his dog ran, Landry replayed the terrifying nightmares in his mind. Like everybody, he'd had other bad dreams, but never ones where he had been trapped and about to die. The creature, a round-bodied thing five feet in diameter with eight thin, hairy legs, could spin silk for a web or a trap. It resembled a spider, but this terrifying monster was unlike anything Landry ever imagined.

Its beady eyes had blazed with a light that pierced into the mind. It could understand your thoughts. Landry told himself how crazy that sounded, but it was true. And the mouth—the gaping maw with a hundred needlelike fangs—resembled no arachnid that ever crawled the Earth.

Granted, he had seen it in a dream, but he had a hunch that the thing existed. That bizarre creature that seemed so real in his dreams was alive—if *alive* was the correct word for such a being.

Sure, people claim the house is the most haunted in town, but could there be some otherworldly creature lurking behind a barricaded door in the ballroom?

There is only one way to find out.

Once he and Simba reached the aquarium, they made a U-turn and headed home. His phone dinged with a text from Cate that said, "Guess you boys are out on the town. When will you be back?"

He replied, "We'll pick up coffee and be home in twenty minutes." He led Simba down a set of concrete steps and walked along Conti Street. At Royal they entered Café Beignet, a dog-friendly establishment with a shady patio Landry and Cate often visited. He ordered coffees and muffins to go, realizing he was about to ruin any benefit he'd gotten from the run, then dismissing that thought with typical Cajun flair. "Life's short and meant to be enjoyed," he said to the little dog trotting by his side. "Let's go feed your mother. I'll bet you're ready for breakfast yourself."

After a shower, he joined Cate on the small balcony off their third-floor bedroom. Simba lay at their feet, watching the activity on St. Philip Street down below. He told her how well their little guy did on his run, and then he switched topics.

"I had two nightmares last night. I'm surprised I didn't wake you." He explained that the scene played out on the top floor of Tartarus House. There was a terrifying spiderlike creature that tied him in lacy strings, and at the end he fell down a staircase. At the point where the beast waited for him to stop struggling against his fibrous bonds, Landry woke up.

"I'm sorry, Cate, but I have to go see what's in that ballroom," he said. "You know me well enough by now to understand how I operate."

"I'm feeling a little déjà vu," Cate replied, struggling to keep calm. "Didn't we discuss this last night? So you dreamed about the old house you were in. Nothing odd about that. You can't go back, Landry. All you'll do is further piss off the guy who lives there. This isn't the first time you've gotten in trouble by acting impulsively, and you must start thinking rationally. You must, Landry. If you don't, you're going to get yourself in serious trouble."

Acting on impulse was a flaw Landry recognized and

accepted; once he had gathered just enough information to see that things might get interesting, he became eager to move. Barging in without thinking had gotten him into serious trouble before, but this was different, or at least he tried to spin it to Cate as different. This was simply an old mansion located just a few blocks over in the French Quarter, and if he got into trouble, help was just a cellphone call away.

"Please don't patronize me," Cate replied evenly. "Since I've known you, we've both seen plenty we can't explain. We know the supernatural exists, and you told me how spooky the house is. Even Simba refused to go near the place, and you know animals have intuitions we don't understand. It's hard to accept that odd stuff is going on right here in the Quarter, but what if you're right? What if there *is* a flesh-eating monster in the attic? Does that make going there a better idea? Hell no, it doesn't. You can't go alone, and that's it."

"Okay, okay. How about this? I'll call Jack. He rescued that girl Angie who was trapped inside. He'll go with me."

"No, Landry, you're not calling Jack. Number one, he's as impulsive as you are. Number two, you'll both end up in trouble. Maybe if we learn more about the house and its owner, we can talk about you going there, but for now, I'm telling you, don't do it."

CHAPTER FIFTEEN

As they walked to work, Landry received a call from Jules Beckman at the Cabildo saying he'd discovered another document relating to the house on Dauphine Street and thought Landry would want to see it. He left Cate and Simba, saying he was going to the museum and would meet them later.

Jules took him to a nearby conference room much larger than his office, where the original drawing they had seen earlier lay unrolled on a table beside another, smaller drawing, as brittle and yellowed as the first, its corners secured by paperweights. Jules wasted no time explaining what he'd found.

"We know the indigo planter Bezaliel Moros built the house in 1723. As it turns out, in 1755 he commissioned an architect to design a remodel of the second floor. I found no reference to a spouse anywhere in my records, and I think he originally built the house expecting to raise a family, but thirty years later he realized that wasn't going to happen. He repurposed four second-floor bedrooms into parlors and a library, added fireplaces and removed closets. The primary suite he left intact, as well as one bedroom at the opposite end of the hall from his for a guest suite. I've laid the two plans side by side for comparison. Take a look, please. Check out the second and third floors. Does anything capture your attention?"

I visited these rooms in my dreams. As Jules had rambled on about the remodeling project, Landry's mind had wandered. Now, being asked to compare the documents, Landry wondered why he was even here. As a courtesy, he gave the plans a cursory glance.

"See anything different?" Jules asked.

"Nothing significant. The 1755 plan has a lot of tiny scribblings inside the perimeters of each room that weren't on the original. I presume those are descriptions of what the rooms will be for, or what they had been."

"They describe the new purposes for the rooms. They're faded and so small they're hard to see. Plus they're in French. These are exciting; one rarely sees floor plans from this period that include room descriptions. I jotted them down so you could more easily read the words."

"Maybe I'm missing something," Landry replied, a little more bluntly than he intended. "Why am I here?"

"Because of this." Jules pointed to the section of the plan that outlined the third floor—the ballroom Jules had described to Landry earlier. "He was also having it repurposed in this 1755 renovation project. Like those extra bedrooms, I guess Bezaliel Moros didn't need a ballroom after twenty-five years as a bachelor."

Landry peered at the newer document. "Do the words inside the perimeter of the room explain its purpose?"

"Oh, yes, they certainly do. Those words are the reason I called you over." He picked up a notepad and read aloud, *"La demure du Monstre mangeur de chair."* He crossed his arms and fidgeted, bursting with excitement as he waited for the obvious follow-up question.

"Which means in English?"

"Literally translated, it says, 'The place where the flesh-eating monster lives.'"

Landry jerked his head up and looked Jules in the eyes. "No shit?" he blurted. "I'm sorry; pardon me. You sure know how to get a guy's attention. Are you certain of the translation?"

"Come with me." Jules led Landry to his office, opened his laptop, and checked for variations of the French words. He searched for what the words would have meant in the eighteenth century, and the conclusion was irrefutable. The meaning was as Jules had said, and Landry sat dumbfounded, staring at the English translation.

"Perhaps it really means 'the place where the people eat meat,' as if he intended to use the room as a banquet hall," Landry suggested, but Jules shook his head. "I'm fluent in French, and I'm confident about the words. *Monstre* means monster, *mangeur* means eater, and *chair* means flesh. If they'd wanted to call the room 'a place where people eat meat,' which would have been an absurd word arrangement, the word for meat-eater would have been *carnivore*, just as it is in English. Not flesh-eater."

Recalling the spiderlike creature from his nightmare, Landry decided not to mention it to Jules yet. "What's he talking about?"

Jules opened both hands palms up in a gesture of bewilderment. "That's your department," he said with a smile. "But tell me one more thing. Do you notice something else familiar on the third floor?"

Landry gave the plan another look. A cavernous main room with six small rooms, likely closets or storerooms, three on each end. Along the long wall on one side was a row of tall windows, and the other was a solid wall except for the door that opened to the stairway, the only means of egress.

The plans were dusty and faded, but as he pored over them, he noticed a small black square in one of the storage rooms. "This looks like the square on the floor plans for our building on Toulouse," he said. "Any ideas yet?"

"None," Jules said. "If we ever learn anything, I'd bet it's going to come from Henri's demolition job instead of by someone snooping around in the ballroom at Tartarus House. You think your building is haunted, but that place puts anything else in the French Quarter to shame."

CHAPTER SIXTEEN

When Landry arrived at the office, he found Henri hard at work. He'd pulled a sofa and chairs away from the wall in a corner that was their reception area, and he stood on a short ladder before a side wall, tape measure in hand, drawing a rectangle on the white plaster. A tarp lay spread on the floor along the wall below him.

"The hidden room had better be back there, because Cate's going to shoot you for scribbling on the wall if it isn't." Landry laughed as he approached Henri. "Are you planning to knock out the plaster?"

"I am. The good news is, as the landlord, I can do whatever damage I wish. Cate's my tenant and has no say; all I'm required to do is restore it to its original condition once I'm finished." He gave Landry a wink, marked a couple more measurements, and stepped off the ladder. "She had little to say when she got here. Pretty much went straight to her office and hasn't ventured out."

"That's on me. We had a huge argument last night about my wanting to go back to Tartarus House. She's mad at me, and if you're about to do what I think you are, having her stay in her office is good news for you. She's not big into demolition or dust or disrupting the norm. Or me right now, for that matter." He saw a hammer on the couch and handed it to Henri. "Are you ready?"

Henri tap-tapped the hammer on the plaster inside the rectangle, and as he moved along, decent-sized pieces fell to the tarp below. Soon he had the area cleared, exposing a network of wood laths covered in the tiny trails made by termites over the decades. He dug out the remaining plaster between the laths and said, "Look! There's an old door hidden behind the wall. This is getting exciting!"

Although he wanted to talk about Tartarus House and his disturbing dreams, Landry understood that now wasn't the time. Henri needed his space; it was rare that he became this enthusiastic about a project, and the thought of finding a passageway built in the early eighteen hundreds, then boarded up and forgotten, excited Landry as well.

Henri removed large sections of the narrow slats, and what lay behind—an ancient, solid wooden door—revealed itself at last. Its knob had been removed when the laths were laid over it, and it was secured with an old-fashioned lock like the one in the door where Angie Bovida had been imprisoned.

"Wonder where I could find a skeleton key these days?" Henri mused, and Landry told him Jack Blair had found an old key in the mansion. "I'm going back there," he added. "I'll look for the stash of keys Jack found and bring you a few."

"No, Landry. I agree with Cate on this one. You mustn't go back now. We must learn more about the house first. Angie Bovida saw a woman, you saw a man, and if his name is Moros as he claims, then he's a descendant. That means it's his house, and you could end up in jail for trespassing. Or worse, depending on what he might really be."

Henri pulled out his phone, looked up a number, and made a call. "Do you sell old skeleton keys?" he asked, breaking into a smile as he heard the answer. "Fine. I'll be around shortly."

"Roche Antiques on Royal, two blocks from here," he said to Landry as he replaced the phone in his pocket. "My project is on hold for the moment, and I don't want to open the door too quickly anyway. I want to savor the thrill of finding a hidden door in my building. Come with me; let's go buy the skeleton key, retire to the Roost, and I can hear about your day over a Sazerac."

Landry told Cate where they were going and asked if she'd join him for dinner at Muriel's. To his surprise, she agreed at once, saying she'd drop Simba at the apartment and meet him there at six. He gave her a thumbs-up and turned to leave when she said, "Don't get your hopes up. We're not done talking just yet." But she waved him off with a smile, which he considered a positive sign.

The Roost Bar lay nestled inside Brennan's, the famous restaurant on Royal Street. Locals knew it well, but most tourists didn't know it existed, and that made it a cozy hideaway for a drink and quiet conversation. Since it wasn't yet four p.m., only a few tables were occupied. They chose a spot in the back of the room, and the bartender, who'd acknowledged their arrival, brought drinks without asking. He understood the routine—these men came here often to talk in undisturbed privacy, and he knew exactly what to do. "Welcome back, Landry, Henri," he said, putting a classic New Orleans Sazerac in front of each of them. "I'll leave you be, but if you need anything else, just whistle!"

Landry explained how his day had gone, beginning with the Cabildo, finding the ancient drawing, and making two trips to the crumbling mansion that might have appeared neglected and abandoned, but in truth was anything but. He described rooms filled with magic paraphernalia—clothing, potions and a plethora of other things—and the man who'd confronted him. Proteus

Moros, the pale, robed man had called himself. Was he a descendant of Bezaliel, the man who somehow still owned Tartarus House three hundred years later?

Landry smiled. "There's something else I want to tell you. I saved the most intriguing for last." He told Henri about the 1755 renovation plan and the French words that described the third-floor ballroom as the home of a flesh-eating monster.

"Fascinating. What do you make of it?"

"I don't know, and that's why I'm so interested in going back. I want to see the ballroom for myself."

Henri said, "The part about the flesh-eating monster sounds ominous enough, but of course it isn't real. There aren't any flesh-eating monsters living in the ballrooms of old French Quarter mansions. Not back in the seventeen hundreds, and not now."

When Landry described his nightmares, Henri's response was like Cate's. Landry had been through a traumatic encounter with a man dressed in costume who stood in a haunted mansion and disclaimed Angie Bovida's tale of being held captive and escaping through a crawl space. That encounter had become fodder for a dream.

"I know you well by now," Henri said sympathetically. "Your desire for knowledge about the paranormal sometimes overpowers your basic instinct for survival. You've been warned that the house is a dangerous place— the most haunted house in a city filled with them. It's true, and until we can discover a way to counteract the power that flows through the mansion, none of us will be safe within its walls."

CHAPTER SEVENTEEN

Landry and Henri parted company on the sidewalk in front of Brennan's when Henri's Uber driver arrived. After having two Sazeracs and spending a stimulating couple of hours listening to Landry's exploits, Henri was ready to go home and relax.

Landry walked the few blocks to Muriel's, where Claude greeted him in the entry hallway and said Cate was sitting at the bar. He took a stool next to her and waved to Kristine, his favorite bartender.

"The usual?" she asked, and he said tonight he'd have what Cate was drinking—a glass of Chardonnay. She poured his, and they chatted for a moment about her recent trip home to St. Louis to visit friends and family. "They're all worried about me being down here in New Orleans with the Harbingers going on," Kristine said. "If anybody knows what it's all about, it'd be you, right?" She waved her hand toward the empty room. "Look at this place. It should be full, but you're the only ones here. People are afraid, Landry. I don't blame them because I'm afraid too."

It was all people talked about, and he commiserated with the plight of every server and bartender and restaurant owner. So far the Harbingers remained a mystery, and Landry said he and his team were doing all they could to unravel the reason they so abruptly began.

Cate clinked his glass, and they talked about the hidden door and his discussions with Henri over drinks. He admitted Henri was as reticent for him to go back to Tartarus House as Cate was. "I guess you got to him," he said with a grin.

"We haven't spoken about it, but how would he feel any other way? There's so much we don't understand about that place, and its reputation as the Quarter's most haunted house goes way back. You understand the paranormal business better than anyone, and it surprises me sometimes how quickly you disregard facts and logic when you're chasing a good story."

He confessed she was right, promised not to do anything without consulting them, and their cocktails and dinner date progressed far better than he had expected. By eight they were in bed with Simba snuggled down between them, surely the most contented dog in the world. At ten it was lights out, and as they kissed goodnight, the dog retired to his crate on the floor with a stretch and a yawn.

The next morning at eight they arrived at the building to find a queue along the sidewalk in front of their building that snaked through the carriageway leading to the pub's patio and their office entrance. As he squeezed through the crowd, several people recognized Landry, and people began shouting his name. When a man grabbed Landry's arm, Simba gave his most ferocious growl and bared his teeth. Landry jerked his arm free with a glare, said "Excuse me!" to two people who were blocking the door that led upstairs to their office, and elbowed them out of the way.

The crowd shouted questions. "What's going on with the Harbingers?" "Why is all this supernatural stuff happening?" "Should people be afraid to celebrate Mardi Gras?"

"We're working on it, but we know nothing more than you. Celebrate Mardi Gras. Support our local businesses, but stay alert. These are strange times."

While he spoke to the crowd, Cate removed a key from her pocket. As they slipped through the door, she pointed to a handwritten sign Henri had tacked up. "VISITORS WILL BE ALLOWED FROM ONE TO FIVE P.M. ONLY."

Now Landry understood the crowd in the hallway. As the Harbingers continued, a steady stream of visitors came to the Paranormal Network to get answers. Yesterday the mob had been in their office, but thanks to Henri's sign and a locked door, now they were relegated to the ground floor.

Landry shut the door and turned the lock as people shoved and knocked and demanded entry. "God, those people are pushy," he muttered. "Even Simba's pissed."

"You can't blame them for being scared. You're the expert; it makes sense they want to talk to you."

Upstairs, Simba trotted straight to his dog bed in Cate's office, turned around three times, lay down, and stretched his long legs with a contented sigh. They joined Henri, who was standing before the door, a piping hot cup of tea in his hand.

"The brewpub on the first floor isn't a happy tenant this morning," Landry quipped. "You solved one problem for us and created another for them."

"Maybe the mob will have breakfast in the courtyard," Henri replied as he held up one of the skeleton keys they bought yesterday. "I've been here since seven, just waiting for you two to arrive so we can open the door. It was hard to be patient, but I wanted all of us to be here when we learn what's inside."

Henri inserted the rusty old key and turned it right and left. When nothing happened, Cate asked, "What do we do next, knock down the door?"

"That won't be necessary. This should do it." Henri pulled two more keys from his pocket. The shop owner had explained there were three basic skeleton keys, one of which will open ninety percent of antique indoor locks. They were considered "master keys" in the eighteenth and nineteenth centuries, and he suggested Henri purchase one of each.

"At two dollars apiece, I couldn't say no," he quipped as he tried the second key, which also didn't work. The third was the charm; when inserted in the keyhole, it was a perfect fit and turned easily to the left. They heard a distinct click as the bolt disengaged, and Henri said, "Voila! Now cross your fingers we can get in without using a crowbar!"

With no knob, they had nothing to tug on. Henri inserted a flathead screwdriver between the door and jamb and tried to pry it open, but nothing worked. They examined the door up and down, and Landry pointed to a narrow opening between the bottom of the door and the floor. "Look at how warped this door is. There's a quarter-inch difference from one side to the other, probably because the floor has settled over the years. I don't think we're going to get it open this way. I think that crowbar you mentioned may not be a bad idea."

An hour later, after exhausting every possibility except destroying the door or jamb, they admitted defeat. Henri went to his office and returned with a pry bar he'd brought from home. They called Phil Vandegriff down from the studio to shoot video. Phil, who was the Paranormal Network's lead cameraman and audio-video guru, had left Channel Nine with Landry when the Paranormal Network launched. Having worked alongside Landry for years, he'd seen enough to be a believer in the supernatural.

Phil set up a tripod and mounted the camera. "Ready," he announced, and Henri pushed one end of the bar into the jamb and applied pressure. Nothing happened on the first few tries, but then the door split with a loud crack, and a large piece of it fell to the floor. Although they still couldn't get inside, at least they might glimpse what lay behind it.

Cate wanted to retrieve a flashlight, but Henri stopped her. "Be patient, both of you. This is my project, and I refuse to rush things. We'll find out what secrets lie behind this door once we remove it."

Another thirty minutes passed as Henri pried off more chunks with the crowbar. At last he used it on the lock, and after a few hard pushes, its mechanism burst open, parts flying everywhere. Henri took hold of the shattered door and gave it a tug. Ancient hinges creaked and groaned with an eerie, haunting noise that signaled the years that had passed since the last time it had been opened.

As Phil went upstairs to get a klieg light, they waited impatiently, staring into blackness so intense they could see nothing past a few feet. Simba trotted over, and despite their frantic calls for him to stop and stay, he walked right inside, disappeared into the gloom, and began barking furiously.

"Phil! Come back! Hurry!" Cate screamed as Landry plunged into the space to rescue his dog. Seconds later the barking stopped, and Landry said, "We're okay. There's…what the hell? The floor's wet. C'mon, boy. Let's go."

Phil aimed the powerful light and flipped a switch. The room became bright just as Landry carried the dog through the door. He put Simba on the floor, felt his wet shoes, and held his fingers to his nose. "Appears to be water," he said. "No taste, no smell, no color."

"How on earth could water be in there?" Henri asked. "Does it cover the floor?"

"I don't think so. I stepped in it and out again, like going through a puddle."

"Look in here, guys," Phil said, pointing through the doorway. With the klieg light installed, they crowded around and saw a thick, hazy mist that filled the room. They could just make out the side and back walls through the fog, and Landry pointed to something on the floor toward the back of the room.

"There's the black square that we saw on the old floor plan. That must be where I stepped in the water. I'll check it out." He took a step through the door, but Cate pulled him back by the sleeve.

"What if that fog is poisonous?" she asked, but he'd already been in it and said it felt like drizzling moisture that clings to your face. He stepped inside, entered the cloud, and they watched his form recede until he was just a hazy figure while only fifteen feet away.

"This is odd," he called out, the mist muffling his words. "This black thing on the floor is like a miniature reflecting pool, an inch or so deep and a couple of feet square. I can see myself in the water. You guys come on in. The water's fine!"

"Har, har," Cate answered, and asked Henri if he thought it was safe.

"From what I can see, he's doing fine, but let's leave someone outside just for safety's sake. Phil, step into the room so you can film us. Cate, if you want to go too, I'll stay out here."

She stepped into the mist, saw Landry kneeling by the black square, walked over and screamed, "My God, there's a face in the water! It's leering at me. Landry, get back!" She bolted out of the room, thinking he'd be right behind her.

"I don't see it," Landry said, leaning over to look more closely. He put his hand into the water, and suddenly he toppled forward and disappeared into the black square. Phil and Henri rushed over, shouting his name. But the water was dark and still and only one inch deep. Landry was gone.

"What happened to him?" Phil yelled. Henri had an idea but kept it to himself for now. "We must tell Cate," he said.

Cate sat in her office, taking deep gulps of air. "That face scared the daylights out of me! I thought I was going to have a heart attack! What the hell is that black square, anyway?"

"Landry's disappeared, Cate," Henri said, his voice trembling with a mix of shock and concern.

"Disappeared?" Her eyes widened in disbelief. "How? I was just with him." The abruptness of Henri's statement sent a shiver down her spine. Panic crept into her voice. "Oh, my God. Did that thing...did he somehow go into that black hole?"

Henri nodded, confirming her worst fears. The room spun as the realization sank in. Cate was gripped by the sheer terror of the unknown—the things Landry Drake did as part of his job. Without a second thought, she sprinted out of her office, ran into the secret room, and dropped to her knees beside the enigmatic square. Her tears flowed like raindrops, and between sobs she muttered, "How? How did it happen, and where is he?"

"I'm so sorry, Cate. I don't know what happened; somehow he got pulled into that black square. It seems only an inch deep, but it has paranormal qualities. We must summon Madame Blue, and we need to do it quickly."

Cate knew whom Henri was referring to, and a glimmer of hope overshadowed her heartache. "Hurry, Henri. Get her over here before something terrible happens to Landry!" Filled with desperation, she clung to a sliver of hope that the noted psychic might hold the key to saving Landry from the mysterious abyss that had swallowed him.

CHAPTER EIGHTEEN

Cate had known Madame Blue for several years. A well-known psychic who first assisted Landry in what became a *Bayou Hauntings* episode called "The Proctor Hall Horror," she was held in high regard by Henri Duchamp, who had worked with her for many years. He considered her one of a handful of legitimate psychics in New Orleans and a person with connections to the supernatural that defied comprehension.

She lived above a small shop on the quiet end of Bourbon Street and didn't need a crystal ball or a pack of tarot cards to see into the past or the future. She had occult powers, and the moment Henri mentioned her name, Cate told herself to stay calm. If anyone could rescue Landry, it would be Madame Blue.

When the seeress heard the urgency in Henri's voice, she dropped everything and rushed to the office. Henri summarized what had happened, and Cate described the malevolent, ghostly face that had stared at her from the black square.

"Take me to where it happened," the psychic said. In the hidden room, she knelt by the square, dipped her fingers into the water, and whispered, "This is a portal, a conduit to a different place, another realm perhaps. I can feel the energy radiating within it."

"I thought as much," Henri replied as doubts crept back into Cate's mind. She wondered if she would ever see Landry again, or if he was lost in a mysterious black void forever. The only thing she knew for certain was that she would stop at nothing to find him and bring him back from the depths of the portal that had swallowed him whole.

Madame Blue stared into the blackness and murmured an incantation in an arcane language. As she spoke, the water rippled, then became a whirling vortex. A face materialized in the water, the one Cate had seen—a menacing countenance with cold, evil eyes and lips that curled into a sneer. Henri gasped as he realized this was no apparition. The being's mouth moved, the nose flared in anger, and its gleaming red eyes locked onto Madame Blue's.

"Appear!" she shouted, her outburst surprising Henri, who took an involuntary step backwards. She cried again, "Appear!"

The whirlpool rose, lifting a figure whose countenance was a pulsating mass of shadows and malevolence. There was a nasty, sickening odor as the outline of a robe took shape, followed by arms and a head. The facial features appeared last—those eyes that gleamed with an unholy light and a twisted, evil smile. Before them stood a tall man whose very essence was the embodiment of hate and wickedness.

Henri withdrew further while Madame Blue stood her ground. "I had an idea it would be you. Where is he, Bezaliel? Where have you taken Landry Drake? I want him back, now!"

As Henri watched, the being spoke, his voice slithering into Henri's mind, taunting him with whispers of deep fears and regrets. He turned his face, and his eyes bored into

Henri's. "Who do we have here? Henri Duchamp, the famous scholar of the paranormal. And Madame Blue, a seeress held in high regard by mortals. We meet again, Madame, but you have forgotten my powers. Never give me an order, you fool. Landry Drake will return when—*if* I say he will return."

"Where is he?"

Bezaliel snarled, "How limited are your powers. If you will but think, you'll realize there's only one place he could be. He passed through the portal, of course. Some call you a great seeress. If that's true, then look into your mind's eye and tell *me* where he is."

She pressed her fingertips to her temples and closed her eyes. "He's somewhere inside Tartarus House. But is he safe?"

"Safe? Yes, for now, but I suppose that depends on my mood. However, *you* can ensure his safety. You and Mr. Duchamp here. There's something I want. Give it to me, and you can have your friend back."

"What do you want?"

"I want the book. Give it to me, and everything will return to normal. The diversions the people call Harbingers will end, and Mr. Drake will no longer be my guest."

Henri said, "I don't know what book you're talking about. I don't have a book…"

Suddenly Bezaliel raised his arms and pointed them at Henri. Brilliant flames flew from his fingertips, and a sudden, enormous gust of wind set the hazy mist and the water in the shallow pool swirling about. He shouted, "Landry Drake dies unless you give me the book!" and stepped into the black square, descending into the whirlpool and disappearing.

Back in the office, Henri asked Madame Blue about the portal, saying he'd read of them but had never seen one. She explained that the black square in the floor was a supernatural passage—a teleportal warp that facilitated movement from one place to another sometimes in time but also in space. One entered the portal as both Landry and Bezaliel had done, and one would emerge on the other side, wherever that was.

"My theory is when they came here ages ago, Bezaliel and Proteus traveled through a portal from another realm and possibly another time as well. The first we hear of Bezaliel was in the early seventeen hundreds, when he was granted the property to build his house. Bezaliel installed a portal at Tartarus House, and it was no coincidence that LaPiere put one here as well."

"Why would he do that?"

"Perhaps Lucas LaPiere became acquainted with Bezaliel when he emigrated to New Orleans. Bezaliel was already here—and probably Proteus as well—and when Lucas LaPiere built his house, this building where we are, in 1803, he added a hidden room and consented to have a portal installed in it."

Henri asked what connection LaPiere and Bezaliel Moros would have had.

"It's voodoo. I'm certain of it. Lucas LaPiere brought hundreds of African and Caribbean men, women, and children to New Orleans, many of whom were imprisoned one floor above where we sit. These people had strong cultural and religious beliefs, and voodoo spread like wildfire in the city. It's still practiced today, but the practitioners keep a low profile. Believe me, it's as powerful in the twenty-first century as it was in the nineteenth.

"I'm certain Bezaliel and Proteus are immortals who would have been students of arcane subjects, and with their powers, they knew that the slaves practiced voodoo. When Bezaliel's new friend Lucas built a building to house his human cargo, Bezaliel wanted a connection to the voodoo that would inevitably run rampant in this building. LaPiere built the portal, and Bezaliel created a supernatural passageway between his house and this one."

"So you think Landry was transported to Tartarus House?"

Madame Blue nodded. "Bezaliel as much as confirmed it. He's inside Tartarus House, but it would be foolhardy to consider using the portal to go there. Portals don't always connect to the same place. If you stepped into that black square now, it might take you to ancient Rome or modern-day China or wherever Bezaliel wanted it to go.

"We must move on. We're wasting time, Henri. Before anything else, we must find the book Bezaliel wants so we can free Landry."

CHAPTER NINETEEN

Landry's eyes fluttered open. For a moment, he wondered if he was still trapped within the confines of his eerie dream or if reality had taken an even darker turn. He lay on the cold, dusty floor of a room bathed in a muted light that seemed to emanate from nowhere. An intricate web of gossamer threads as delicate as spider silk but far stronger constrained his arms and legs.

Frantically, Landry attempted to piece together his fragmented memories. He recalled being in that hidden room Henri uncovered at the office, bent over the enigmatic black square. It beckoned to him, drawing him into its abyss with flashes of dazzling light and the haunting notes of music he couldn't quite identify. It was as though he had been hurtling through space at breakneck speed while at the same time floating on a tranquil sea.

In seconds he ended up here on the top floor of the ancient mansion. Like the one at the office, a black square lay nestled within a nearby closet. How much time passed since he arrived here? Hours, perhaps even days? He didn't know, as time lost its meaning in this surreal place. Weakness washed over him, every muscle and joint in his body aching as if he had been subjected to an otherworldly ordeal.

As he lay bound by wispy filaments, Landry couldn't shake the feeling that someone—or something—was watching. He strained his eyes, attempting to pierce the shadowy corners of the room, but he could see nothing beyond the eerie, ethereal threads that held him captive.

He clung to a glimmer of hope: whatever ensnared him in this fiendish trap didn't appear to be in the room. This respite, however, was short-lived as he recalled his chilling dream. In it, he had been ensnared and immobilized just as now, and the only escape had been a frantic tumble down a narrow stairway. Dangling from the ceiling above hung the nightmarish creature—spindly, spiderlike, and infinitely patient. It waited for him to cease his struggles, biding its time with a malevolence that sent shivers down Landry's spine.

The memory of that nightmarish event drove Landry to the brink of madness. His body writhed in spasms, and he screamed in unbridled fear. It was a momentary lapse, a desperate outburst that he instantly regretted.

The moment he cried out, a sinister hissing echoed from high above, and Landry realized his earlier assumption had been a grave error. The creature had been here all along, lurking in the shadows of the enormous ballroom.

As the hissing persisted, Landry's heart pounded in his chest. Just as in his horrifying dream, it waited with inhuman patience for him to falter, to surrender to fear. In this nightmarish mansion, trapped within a sinister web, Landry became locked in a deadly game of survival against an enigmatic and malevolent force that defied comprehension.

CHAPTER TWENTY

The haunting incidents in the French Quarter grew more severe as Mardi Gras day approached. A man walking his German shepherd dog on Bourbon Street suddenly released the animal, commanding him to attack four college girls who were approaching. As the coeds stood transfixed in horror, the vicious beast leapt into the air, flying toward them with fangs bared and lips drawn back into a fierce grimace. Believing they were about to be torn to shreds, they fell to the pavement. They cowered in fear, but just as the animal reached them, the beast and his master vanished, leaving the intended victims screaming and asking police how and why this happened. Was the dog real? Was it a cruel trick—a prank for Carnival? The answers would never come.

A far more frightening and sinister event happened in an antebellum mansion very near the cathedral and the Cabildo. On the Wednesday before Mardi Gras, an elaborate costume party was in full swing. The hosts were Dr. and Mrs. Doucet, a prominent local banker and her physician husband, who held court dressed as the Bonapartes, Napoleon and Josephine. Four dozen guests admired each other's regalia, tried to guess who was who, and sipped Salon de Mesnil Brut champagne, the 2002 vintage, of course, which cost a thousand dollars a bottle. It was Carnival season, and nothing but the best would do for the wealthy and their guests.

"Who is that?" one invitee asked his hostess, nodding toward an imposing figure dressed as a magician who glided silently among the others. She didn't know, nor had anyone noticed his arrival. The man, presuming it was a man, stood at least six and a half feet tall and held a wand in one hand. He wore a conical black hat, and his robe was adorned with tiny half-moons and stars that twinkled.

Battery-operated, I'd guess, one society matron sniffed to another. *A little tacky for an affair such as this, don't you think?*

The figure appeared more menacing because of a grotesque mask that covered his face and added an aura of mystery. It had a long, pointed nose in what Orleanians called "plague doctor" style, and within dark sockets, his eyes glowed crimson. Garish colors ran down the cheeks of his mask, and the lips were painted blood red.

How does he see with those glowing red lights in the eyeholes?

He can't even take a drink while wearing a mask that covers his mouth. What's the point? He has to take off the mask eventually, right?

Who the hell is he?

While the guests sashayed about in their vibrant masks and elaborate costumes, mingling with their friends and enjoying a respite from the Harbingers, the mysterious figure stood alone. Those in attendance had given up trying to learn his identity. He never spoke a word, and with every passing hour the guests felt more uneasy. Something was off about the man who moved about the room in silence as though assessing his fellow guests. Some of them put in a quiet, anxious word with the hosts.

Mrs. Doucet stepped into the study, checked the guest list, and accounted for everyone but him. As midnight drew near and the celebration reached its crescendo, the hostess decided it was time to solve the mystery. She turned to her husband and said, "Find out who he is, darling. This is our home, and I think he's crashed our soirée. If he has, kick his ass out." Fueled by alcohol, Dr. Doucet agreed, but out of caution he went to the foyer and spoke to the plainclothes security guard they'd hired. The men strode across the room and approached the tall figure. The doctor said, "Who are you, sir? You have an excellent costume, but we can't identify you, and everyone's wondering."

A deep laugh issued from behind the mask, and the red eyes glowed bright and steady. Still the man said nothing.

"If you won't remove your mask immediately, I'm afraid I must ask you to leave."

Another boisterous laugh, not jolly but harsh and mocking. There was something repellent and forbidding about the man, and Dr. Doucet stepped back. The figure turned away, but the security guard stopped him, taking hold of his arm and reaching to remove his mask.

Seconds later, shouts and screams and calls to 911 filled the beautiful home on Orleans Avenue. Partygoers in full costume spilled out into the street, trying to distance themselves from the horror unfolding inside. A block away on Bourbon Street, mounted officers assigned to crowd control heard the commotion and rushed to the scene.

The cops flew through oversized double doors that stood wide open. Before them lay the great room, where moments earlier a party had been underway. Bodies lay strewn about the room, some unmoving and others writhing in pain or screaming for help. Every surface—the furniture and walls and paintings, and even the guests—dripped with mucus and blood. In the center of the room lay a pile of flesh and bone that resembled a carcass at a slaughterhouse. Officers struggled to keep down their dinner while trying to learn what had happened, but as one knelt to talk to a costumed guest on the floor, he felt something hitting his arm.

Drip. Drip. Drip.

Horrified, he tried to brush away the drops of red liquid, but more fell. As he looked up, one hit him squarely on the cheek. His shout for help became a gurgle as he vomited, and he became so light-headed he struggled to move himself from under the bloody, dripping corpse that lay draped in the arms of a massive chandelier fifteen feet above.

Many of the officers who worked the scene that night were seasoned veterans. Others were rookies, but they all took it hard. They walked into carnage of a magnitude none of them had seen. Each was so shaken that counselors would work with them for weeks afterwards. Some recovered and returned to the force; some couldn't get past it and didn't. One committed suicide.

Most of the guests at the party survived, and once they were able to speak of the horror they witnessed, they gave similar accounts about what happened. Some things had to be left to conjecture, but the authorities pieced together a generally accurate and mostly complete story.

Their host and a private security guard had been talking to the mysterious man people had whispered about all evening. They were standing in the center of the room under the chandelier, and as the man turned away, the guard took his arm and reached up to remove the man's mask.

With a flick of the wand held tightly in the figure's gloved hand, a flash of blinding light erupted, and an ear-piercing explosion shook the ballroom. The security guard, at whom the wand was pointed, suddenly blew apart, his guts and blood and bones flying everywhere, spattering every surface with greasy gore.

Dr. Doucet, who was still standing next to the figure,

reached out to take the wand and stop the man from using it again, but the figure pushed him backwards to the floor, pointed the baton at him, and raised it in an arc, causing the doctor's body to rise into the air and float up to the chandelier. It hovered for a moment before the eyes of the terrified guests, then crashed onto the sharp metal spikes that formed the fixture's arms. Impaled there, he twisted and screamed as his blood dripped onto the parquet floor below. Within moments he was dead.

Panic ensued as people scrambled to escape the chaos. Younger guests knocked aside older ones, trampling them while fleeing the carnage. What had been a glamorous ball destined for the society pages became the lead story on every news source—a scene of devastation and horror with bodies everywhere, tables and chairs scattered, and the haunting echoes of screams filling the air.

It was this party held during the week before Mardi Gras that left a lasting scar on the community, hurtling Carnival into a terrifying cloud of uncertainty. The public panicked when it learned that the mysterious figure was nowhere to be found; during the mayhem he had vanished as suddenly as he'd appeared hours earlier. The police chief's promise that the man would be apprehended was of no solace to the jittery population, many of whom had already decided they couldn't stomach any more Harbingers.

"This perpetrator may still be in the city," the chief said in an early morning news conference. "He didn't disappear into thin air. He slipped out of the house during the chaos. Someone knows who this man is, where he lives, and what makes him tick, and I implore you to call the police if you see anything suspicious. There's a reasonable explanation for everything that happened, and we will get to the bottom of it."

A city on edge wanted to take comfort in the chief's statement, but many natives whose families had lived in

New Orleans for generations knew his words weren't true. In the Big Easy, not everything could be efficiently packaged and tied up with a reasonable explanation. Things happened here that defied the imagination, but the Harbingers—the scary, unexplainable events in the days before Mardi Gras—had suddenly intensified in the most horrific manner. Locals had taken in stride the disappearing man in a bar and even the mysterious float of the nonexistent Krewe of Moros. NOLA was a spooky city, after all, and crazy stuff like voodoo was part of its culture.

But the tragedy that had played out at the Mardi Gras party would neither be taken in stride nor forgotten. The people would demand answers that the authorities couldn't provide, and the level of fear in New Orleans would magnify with each passing day.

CHAPTER TWENTY-ONE

After founding the Louisiana Society for the Paranormal decades earlier, Henri had accumulated a vast trove of ancient and esoteric books that resided in an enormous library in the building next door. The books had been carefully cataloged and entered into a database, and researchers and students alike could often be found in one of several carrels, exploring one of the world's most comprehensive collections of the arcane and supernatural.

In the time since Landry disappeared, Henri had spent the rest of that day and all night at his office, scrolling through the database as he tried to find the book Bezaliel wanted. He'd hand it over; no book was worth endangering his friend and partner, but he'd see Landry free before he did so.

Cate was in a frenzy. Hours had slipped away since Landry's disappearance, leaving her in a state of agonizing uncertainty if he'd ever come back to her. Madame Blue had advised against contacting the police, as the disappearance of the paranormal investigator would heighten the fears of the residents. If he could enter the portal, then the psychic was certain he could return through it. Would he be able to do so? That was a question Madame Blue had kept to herself.

Consumed by her anguish, Cate sat on the floor in the secret room, her beloved boy Simba by her side, gazing into the unfathomable depths of the one-inch-deep square of water. Her tears flowed as the dog licked her hand, hoping to cheer her up.

Cate was no quitter. While she wondered if she'd be forever separated from the man she loved, her determination remained unwavering. For now, the only certainty in her life was her unyielding resolve to spare no effort in rescuing Landry from the abyss that had sucked him down. She didn't know how, but she would keep working with the others to unravel the mysteries of the portal. At last she stood, hooked Simba's leash to his collar, and took him home.

After a sleepless night, Cate and Simba arrived at the office before sunrise, hoping to hear that Henri had made progress, but it wasn't to be. When she walked in, he stood, stretched and said, "I need to go home and take a shower. I've gotten nowhere in the past twelve hours, and I think I've been looking in the wrong place."

"Go get some sleep," she said. "Simba and I will hold things down here. Your no-visitor sign is still posted downstairs, and that'll keep things quiet for a while. I'll be fine until you get back." Once he left, she sat at her desk and racked her brain to think where a book might be. She looked everywhere in the office, then went up to the production studio and rummaged around to be sure an old volume hadn't been misplaced. When she returned, she walked into the hidden room.

She said, "Landry, help me out here. I want you back, and I'm worried about you. If you'll give me a sign, I'll look anywhere you say." She tried to clear her brain to make it receptive, but it was impossible not to think of him. Several minutes passed with no answers, but when she turned to leave, a thought popped into her head. The secret door had been covered with the same plaster as the walls inside the hidden room. *What if...*

She closed her eyes, and this time she prayed not for Landry's help but for God's guidance. She chose a corner and began knocking with her fist as she moved down the wall. Rapping constantly, she walked along until she reached the far corner. The walls seemed solid, but she kept going because she had no other plan. She covered the second wall—the back one—and made the turn to work her way down the third wall. Becoming discouraged, she rapped and heard a hollow echo. Something was behind the plaster. *A space! Let it be a space!*

Cate retrieved Henri's hammer, told herself he'd forgive the destruction if she was on the wrong track, and began rapping on the plaster. Small chunks fell to the floor, and soon she had created an opening. It was a space between the bricks, twelve inches square and ten deep. Most of it was empty, which created the hollow echo, but in the bottom was a wooden box and something wrapped in a ragged cloth.

As her heart raced, she murmured a quick thanks to God and removed the box and the thing wrapped up under it. The moment she touched it, the cloth disintegrated into a pile of dust, revealing two ancient books.

One of these may free Landry! She gasped as she carried the three items from the hidden room into the office. Knowing Henri might not return until the afternoon, she made a decision, knowing he would forgive her for acting without consulting him. She called Madame Blue and revealed what she'd found.

The excited psychic arrived in only a few minutes. Cate showed her the hidden space inside the secret room and the three things she had found inside. Madame Blue said she didn't know who might have hidden the items, but given the secret cache and its proximity to the portal, she was optimistic Cate might have found what Bezaliel was after.

The books and the box lay on the conference table where Cate had placed them. The volumes were old and brittle, their bindings crudely fashioned out of some material she didn't recognize. Realizing how fragile they were, Cate had left them alone, and she watched with interest as the seeress pulled a pair of white cotton gloves from her pocket, put them on, and placed the larger of the books before her.

Phil Vandegriff walked through at that moment, stopped by to check on progress, and once he saw what they were up to, he asked them to give him five minutes. Shortly he returned with recording equipment, gave the OK sign, and Madame began describing the book. Cate watched her, noting the excitement in her voice and the trembling of her hands. For the jaded psychic to be this enthralled, Cate knew it was an important moment.

"This is an ancient book bound in some type of animal skin. It has no name on the spine, but look at this icon on the cover. It's a large oval eye, which reminds me of the Eye of Providence found on the back of a dollar bill. I'd say the similarity ends there because that eye symbolizes God's protection over the new nation. I believe I know what this book is, and if I'm right, there's nothing godly in it."

She turned to the frontispiece—a faded color rendition of the same eye—and the title page, which contained two lines of foreign words.

Τα μυστικά των αρχαίων

Arcana Antiquorum

"The top line is Greek, and the second is Latin. The English translation is *The Secrets of the Ancients*."

"You can read ancient Greek?" Cate whispered.

"I recognize the Greek words only because I have seen them before and because the Latin translation appears on the next line. Latin is a language in which I am fluent. I have come across references to this book in my studies, although I never expected to see it or touch it. It's unique, priceless and quite old—older even than the time of Christ."

Cate sat dumbfounded as Madame Blue carefully turned a few pages and looked at the entries. "All in Latin, as I had hoped," she murmured as she then mouthed words without speaking. After studying a few pages, she leaned back in her chair and said, "This is the most fascinating thing I have ever beheld, and in my career, I have seen some amazing things."

"What is it, and is it what Bezaliel wants?"

"Let me put it this way. It's a book of secrets beyond mortal comprehension. It contains knowledge of forgotten curses and long-lost incantations. In today's vernacular, it's a book of magic spells, but that description doesn't do it justice. In the wrong hands, this book is unbelievably dangerous. Each page carries words bearing risks and consequences. The spells are real, and without a deep understanding of magical principles, any misstep, or mispronunciation of the Latin words—even voicing them can lead to catastrophic results.

"Does Bezaliel want this book? Perhaps, but we must never allow him to get his hands on it."

CHAPTER TWENTY-TWO

Cate's nerves had been stretched to breaking since Landry's disappearance yesterday. The tantalizing thrill of finding a secret book that might secure his freedom had buoyed her sagging spirits. But now, with a single utterance, Madame Blue had dashed her hopes.

The words spilled from her lips in a rush of frustration and disbelief. "We can't just hand over the book to Bezaliel? What the hell are you talking about? Of course we can, and we must, because that's the key to saving Landry's life. Why would you even—"

"Please, my dear, just wait a moment," the psychic interrupted gently. "The book isn't the sole answer to resolving Landry's predicament. We'll discuss everything with Henri, of course, and I'll explain why I said what I did. Let's finish what we're doing here first."

Carefully, Madame Blue picked up the second book, which seemed more like an artifact on the brink of disintegration, a collection of brittle pages bound in some kind of animal skin with a blank cover. She turned to the first page and gasped, "Oh my goodness," as the two words on the title page registered in her mind. "This book eclipses the other, and it might be one of the most important discoveries in history. How it came to be here is an enigma, but I must retract my earlier statement. This book and not the other is what Bezaliel is after."

She turned a few brittle pages and read the faded words with a mix of wonder and excitement. Her voice quivered as she whispered, "I've heard of this book, of course. Everyone in my field has. But it's been lost since the days of the pharaohs. This can't be the original because books didn't exist in those times. Someone transcribed it from an ancient scroll. That said, this volume you found may itself be thousands of years old."

Unable to contain her curiosity any longer, Cate smiled and said, "How much longer are you going to keep me in suspense?"

Lost in thought, Madame Blue looked at her blankly, then offered an apology. "I was carried away for a moment. Rarely does one find herself in the presence of something truly extraordinary. This is the *Secreta Aeternitatis,* or *Secrets of Eternity*. The book first appears in the works of Hesiod, a Greek poet who lived twenty-five centuries ago. Hesiod describes a book penned by the ancients—the gods of mythology—which holds the legendary secrets to creation, existence and the balance between mortal and divine realms.

"Scholars considered it fiction because it is said the words can unravel the mysteries of the cosmos and allow one to understand the intricate threads that interplay between the gods and mortals. These are complex and mysterious subjects, so let me simplify it: this book contains the secrets to unparalleled power. This might, however, provide the solution to all our problems."

"How is that?"

"I'd prefer not to speculate until I can examine it more closely. I'd like to take both with me if I may. I can translate the Latin, but I will need the computer to unravel the meaning of the arcane passages. More importantly, with the book in my possession, I have the power to protect it from Bezaliel."

"Why does he want it?"

"He is a vain, envious creature who will never be satisfied until he becomes the dominator of the mortal world. He's been at this for millennia, and his defeats have caused other gods to spurn and mock him. I believe this book contains secrets that would allow Bezaliel to unravel the threads that maintain the cosmic balance. By doing so, he could bring himself to equal footing with his divine counterparts—his godly adversaries. His obsession with power blinds him to what he may cause, uprooting the mortal world and rending the fabric of reality itself. I he gets the book and performs the spells, the entire world could end. In that scenario, he loses everything, but so does humanity. We must not let that happen."

Madame Blue's gaze drifted toward the unassuming small wooden box, and a spark of excitement lit her eyes as she unlatched and opened it. The size of a common shoebox, its contents held the promise of something extraordinary. Within it lay five enigmatic objects, each radiating an aura of mystery.

She exclaimed, "This is utterly captivating! What a remarkable treasure trove you've found. First the extraordinary books, and now these objects. They're tools a sorcerer might employ. Each has a special purpose and paranormal properties. I can't begin to estimate their age or to whom they belonged. Let's delve into each one, and I'll explain as best I can what their purposes might be."

She took out a crystal, inside of which burned a small flame. "This one is easy to identify. It's perpetual fire; despite having no fuel, this flame will burn until extinguished by the power of an identical orb. This relic can provide heat and light and has healing properties. It also serves as a beacon to guide those moving between the

Earth and the immortal realms." Carefully replacing the crystal, she removed a deck of tarot cards. In addition to the usual mystical drawings, on each card was written a phrase in Latin. "Each of these contains a powerful curse or a blessing," she explained. "They must not be read aloud until I learn how they work. Otherwise, one might unleash mysterious properties that have remained locked away for millennia."

The third relic was a beautiful feather quill, its colors brilliant even after so many years. "I've read about this, but I never believed it could be real. It's a quill made from the feather of a phoenix, the mythical, immortal bird," the psychic whispered as she ran her gloved fingers over the object. "The ancients believed that words written with this quill would come true. A person's fondest hopes and wishes—or their darkest curses—will be realized, but the more powerful the request, the higher the cost to its maker." She laid it back in its place, taking a moment to gaze on its beauty before letting it go.

Next she held up a beautiful relic—an ancient amulet on a gold chain. "Amazing!" Madame Blue exclaimed as she ran her fingers over its surface. "I've read of these but never knew if they were real. It's called a Luminarion, supposedly crafted by an ancient civilization long forgotten in the mists of time. It contains deep mystic power, Cate; look at the faint glow it emits and the crystal star suspended in its center.

"This star is a reservoir of pure untamed light. It requires an incantation to activate, and it glows brighter and brighter as one speaks the words before emanating one searing burst of pure white light."

"I don't understand. What's its purpose?"

"It has a dual purpose. As the light shines, the one holding the Luminarion receives a surge of cosmic energy that renders them temporarily invincible. When the light strikes a target, it swirls like ethereal chains, growing ever tighter and causing the victim to recoil in agony as raw energy unravels its very essence."

"Fascinating," Cate said. "But do you only get one shot at your target?"

"I imagine if it were used properly, one shot is all one would need." She replaced the amulet into the box.

The last item was an orb about two inches in diameter. It contained a milky, swirling mist, and when Madame Blue plucked it out and held it in her hand, she looked up at Cate, her eyes wide with surprise, and cried, "Oh my goodness!" before tossing it back as if it were too hot to handle.

"What happened?" Cate asked as Madame Blue shook her head and took a deep breath.

"That one scares me," she said at last. "These remarkable artifacts have long been dismissed as fantasy and folklore. Students of the dark arts scoff at the idea they might exist, or that they possess magical properties. Yet these extraordinary objects lie before us. Among them, the one I just showed you is particularly dangerous. It's called a dreamcatcher.

"The dreamcatcher possesses an uncanny power. When held, it grants the beholder the ability to peer into the deepest recesses of another's mind, revealing their thoughts and intentions. Just moments ago, as I held it aloft, its magic surged through me, and I glimpsed into your thoughts, Cate. You intend to hand over that book to Bezaliel regardless of whether I agree."

She nodded. "What you saw is the truth. It's all I can think about right now, and I'll do anything to get him back."

Cate took Madame Blue's hands in her own. "Thank you for coming and for providing a fascinating assessment of the things I found. I really appreciate your help and your involvement with all of this. Having your insight into the paranormal will be immensely helpful in deciding how to deal with Bezaliel and Proteus. I know little about them—what they are, where they came from and all that—but I am going to give him the book. I know you asked to take it with you and examine it, but I can't allow that. I want to be respectful and cognizant of all the help you have given us. We couldn't have done it without you thus far, but you can't have the book."

Madame Blue replied, "I understand your wanting to help Landry; if my loved one were being held captive by a monster, I'm sure my feelings would be raw as well. I said earlier there may be other ways to deal with Landry's situation than handing over the book. You have been told almost nothing about Bezaliel and Proteus, and now you've uncovered an old manuscript that could be devastating in the wrong hands.

"There's so much more about these two you still don't know. Let me reveal the rest so we may make an informed decision about Landry's imprisonment. Fix me a cup of coffee, and let's get started."

During the brief break, Phil checked his camera. He knew Landry would want him to capture every detail of their efforts to thwart Bezaliel and Proteus, and he wouldn't miss even one of Madame Blue's words.

CHAPTER TWENTY-THREE

Cate brought three coffees back to the conference room and said, "I know what you're about to tell me is important, but every minute that passes is a minute something awful may be happening to Landry. I have an idea. Can Bezaliel or Proteus be in two places at the same time?"

"Not to my knowledge."

"Then lure them both here, and I'll go to the house on Dauphine Street and rescue Landry."

"I wish it were that simple. Although I doubt they can be in two places at once, they have the power to change locations instantly. We could lure them here, but if they had an inkling there was a problem at Tartarus House, they would return so quickly that neither you nor Landry would have time to escape. Let's talk for a bit, and hopefully we can begin to develop a workable strategy."

As Cate and the psychic talked, on the top floor of the decaying mansion a few blocks away, a frantic Landry tried to formulate a plan of his own. Encircled from ankles to neck in loose filaments, he could move his arms and legs a bit, but freeing himself was impossible. He was a mummy lying on the floor, but at least he was alone. He hadn't seen the spiderlike creature from his dreams, although the gossamer strings were a spine-chilling reminder that the monster had plans for him.

He tried to recall every minute of time he'd spent here. Now he lay on the floor in the large ballroom, but earlier he had been in a closet, lying next to a black square identical to the one at his office.

Where is that closet? He lay near the center of the lengthy room, and he saw doors on both ends, six in all. All but one was closed; could that be it? He was at least thirty feet away, and given his incapacitation, he didn't know how he could maneuver there. But he had to try.

With considerable effort, he bent his knees a few inches. If he then pushed his legs back straight, his body moved perhaps three inches. He tried the maneuver once, and again; given his constraints, it was both difficult and tiring, and after two attempts, he was a mere six inches closer to his goal. He took a break, worrying that wasting time might allow the creature to return. Proteus Moros. Landry thought the shape-shifting god might be that creature, and the next time they met might be the end for him.

What do I do if I can get to the closet?

How do I get there? If I can do the contortion move four times in an hour, that's twelve inches of progress. One foot down, twenty-nine or so feet to go. In twenty-nine hours, I'll be at the closet door. But if he comes back before then, I'll be playing Little Miss Muffet with a spider.

Or maybe I'll be dead.

I must make this happen faster. But how?

He spent two more hours sidling along the floor until he came across the thing that might be his salvation. He bent his knees, extended his legs with a mighty push, and cried out in pain. Something had pierced his leg. Inside the gauze, he moved his fingers to touch the spot. Through a tear in his pants he felt liquid. Not much—he wouldn't bleed to death, but it meant he had slid his leg over something protruding from the floor.

Something that might slice through strands of filmy gossamer.

Landry patted the floor with his hand until he found the thing he'd hit—a floorboard nail that had worked loose, its head protruding a few millimeters above the wooden floor. Just enough to snag his leg. And maybe just enough to tear the filament.

He amended his goal; the aim now was to slide back and forth, back and forth until enough of the threads were torn that he could move. He concentrated on his legs; if he could rip off the gauze below his knees, he'd be able to push himself along toward that closet. He felt the nail once again, moved with his butt and his knees to position himself, and pushed his legs down hard against the floorboards. Then he moved up and back, hoping that the nail was snagging the threads. He kept at it until his muscles ached, and when he stopped, he tried to move his hands to feel between his legs, but there wasn't sufficient room.

After a ten-minute rest, he extended his legs to either side to learn if the strings had broken. Nothing felt different, so he started the process once again, painstakingly moving up and back over the nail until his muscles couldn't take it any longer. He took another break, and this time he fell asleep. When he awoke, the room was dark, and he wondered how long he had slept. No matter. He had to keep trying.

Another session was followed by a brief rest, then a third attempt to stretch his legs sideways. This time he felt the gossamer give a little. His plan worked! Adrenaline rushed through his body as he gave another valiant push of the legs, and suddenly he felt a rip. He was free below the knees! He flipped onto his back, bent his knees and pushed himself along the floor until he reached the closet door.

The darkness inside was absolute, and he had nothing to go on but a vague, dreamlike recollection of being next to a black square on the floor. Nevertheless, he had to press on. He pushed himself through the open door and into the small room. Moving along headfirst while propelled by his knees and feet, he felt liquid on his head and neck. At last he had found the black square, and he prayed the rest of his plan would work.

He gave one more mighty push until he felt liquid on his collar and the back of his shirt, and seconds later he felt his body being sucked into the void. He closed his eyes and allowed himself to slide into the black space.

CHAPTER TWENTY-FOUR

Landry looked around, trying to get his bearings in a place of absolute darkness.

Where am I, and how did I get here?

He touched his face, felt dampness, and remembered the water in the black square. He'd been a prisoner, but now he was able to move his arms and legs. The filaments that bound him had disappeared.

A portal. There had been one at the office, and the other side was in the ballroom at Tartarus House. He had come through it, and, convinced that Proteus was going to kill him, he escaped by going back.

But something was terribly wrong. Instead of returning to the office, he sat in a forbidding place where the darkness was all-encompassing and the air heavy with the weight of unfulfilled dreams and missed chances.

Where am I? I left from the office, but what is this place? It is absolutely dark, like being at the bottom of a cave. I can't hear or smell anything. I am lying on a hard, smooth surface that's as cold as ice, and I feel the water of the portal next to me, but those are the only things I sense. Everything else is a void, and I am completely isolated from everything I know.

He sat up and extended his arms, but he touched nothing. He stood, took a few steps in the darkness, then a few more. As panic swept over him, he began running. Faster and faster, he raced forward until he collapsed to the floor, gasping for air. He caught his breath and forced himself to remain calm, and as he ran his hand over the smooth, icy surface, he felt something...familiar.

The water in the portal.

How is this possible? I ran at full speed for enough time to get winded. No barriers impeded me—no walls or doors or anything at all. It was just my feet hitting solid ground, but for how far? Hundreds of feet? At least that many. When I could run no more, I fell to the floor, gasping for air.

And I'm sitting by the portal, precisely where I was before.

I ran hard for five minutes or more without turning or circling or veering to one side. So how can I be back where I started?

What the hell is this place?

A lump formed in his throat. *Hell? Is that where the hell I am?*

I thought by going into the portal once again, I'd end up back in Henri's building. But the portal doesn't link just Tartarus House and our building. It can take you to other places. Places like this one, where there is no reality, no communication, nothing at all.

How do I get back? If I dare use the portal again—if it even works now—where's my next destination?

Alone with his thoughts in absolute darkness, in a place where time seemed to stand still and distance meant nothing, Landry became overwhelmed with sadness and a longing for what might have been. Vivid scenes from his past played in his mind. His father gave Landry a wave as he backed their 1993 Olds out of the driveway in

Jeanerette. His father had died of cancer when Landry was eight, but he was so real and so close that Landry waved back. Decisions haunted him—that event that got him fired from the sheriff's office, the times he ignored Cate's warnings and got into trouble—and unsolved regrets. He loved Cate, and now he also loved their new puppy, although he had told her he didn't want Simba. He needed to listen more and stop the half-baked ideas that put him where he was right now—sitting in a place of nothingness with tears running down his face and trying to get home.

Trembling with fear, he decided his only move was to return through the portal. It might take him back to Tartarus House, where he faced certain death, but he had to try. Perhaps he'd end up where he desperately wanted to go and perhaps not, but he couldn't stay in this place. The introspective torment of the darkness was eating away at his heart and soul, tearing him apart inside. He would go mad here if he didn't get away soon.

Landry ran his fingers through the shallow water and along the sides of the perfect square. Even without seeing, he knew it was black and the water was shimmering. Mustering every ounce of courage and praying this step didn't take him further into this hellish world of darkness, he stepped into the water.

Ready for the overpowering suction that would draw him down, he waited, but nothing happened. He stamped his feet in the inches-deep pool and flailed his arms, trying to make something happen. "Dammit!" he shouted. "Get me out of here!"

In a sudden rush, Landry was sucked into the water and hurled through a bizarre pathway of flashing lights and blaring sounds. In seconds the dizzying sensation of speed overcame him, and he lost consciousness.

He awoke in a room lying on the floor beside a black square. His senses had returned: he saw sunlight filtering through an open door a few feet away. Chunks of plaster lay scattered on the floor beside him, and his heart jumped as he looked up and saw that someone had uncovered a hidden space in the wall.

Is it possible that I'm back?

From somewhere nearby came the sound of voices— ones he recognized! Thank God he had returned to the hidden room on Toulouse Street. Rising to his feet, he prayed a silent thanks as he walked through the door into familiar surroundings.

Cate and Madame Blue sat in the conference room, and as he walked toward them, Simba ran out of Cate's office, squealing with delight and wagging his tail furiously. Landry knelt and hugged the dog tightly as he wiggled in his arms. Cate glanced up and ran to him screaming, "Landry! You're free! How on earth…" She put her arms around his neck and kissed him deeply while Simba licked his face in pure ecstasy.

"Boy, you're in big trouble," she chided as tears streamed down her cheeks. "I thought I'd have to come get you. Come sit with us and tell us what happened."

Cate put Landry in a chair next to hers while Simba curled up beside his feet. Madame Blue was most interested in hearing about Proteus and the spider being that he had shifted into, the gossamer filaments that became his bonds, and how he escaped into a place of darkness.

"Purgatory, if I had to guess," the psychic said. "A place of nothingness and regret and lost opportunity. Or maybe Hell, although I picture Hell as a little more…well, frenzied, but who knows? Regardless, I think you should consider yourself lucky to have returned. And now that Landry's saga has ended, I hope you'll let me take the books, Cate. I need them both, and I promise they will be safe in my hands."

"What books?" Landry asked, and Cate said she'd explain everything later. "Thank God you're back," Cate said, giving him an enormous hug. "We're not doing those kinds of adventures anymore. Right, baby? You've put me through things like this so many times in the past, and I'm tired of being scared. You can't imagine how much I worry about you. Please, please promise me you'll settle down."

Landry smiled, reached down to pat Simba's head, and said, "I'm exhausted, Cate. Simba and I are going home to take a long nap. We can talk about it later."

CHAPTER TWENTY-FIVE

It wasn't yet four p.m. when Landry and Simba arrived back at the apartment, and by the time they were home, the tension and fear that had gripped Landry left him exhausted. He stripped off his clothes, climbed into bed, and called Simba to join him. He closed his eyes and lay awake, thinking about the portal and its purpose, who built it, and if it was being used today. At some point, his conscious, waking thoughts morphed into the alternate realm, and Landry slipped from wakefulness to the welcoming embrace of sleep. Exhausted, he fell asleep recalling what he'd learned from his terrifying journey through the portal. The mysterious void was connected not only to Tartarus House but to the place of darkness. Could there be more such locations, like stations on a subway line? Who created it? Bezaliel?

Something moved in his bedroom, although the ever-watchful Simba continued to nap. That meant it was another dream, which gave him peace as he saw the ancient figure standing a few feet away. Despite no breeze, the inky folds of his robe swayed, and his voice reverberated in a disconcerting mélange of whispers and echoes.

"You wonder about the portal," Bezaliel rasped.

"How long have you been here?"

"Long enough to read your thoughts. Your friend Henri Duchamp is the current guardian of the house Lucas LaPiere constructed. I was there long before any of you were born. I guided Lucas as he built it, imparting enough secrets of the dark arts to arouse his curiosity and make him mine."

"You built Tartarus House in 1723. How old are you?"

He shrugged, twisting his lips into a sneering grin. "Age is a mortal thing that is irrelevant to my kind."

"How did the house survive the Great Fire of 1788, when most of the city was destroyed?"

"Proteus," Bezaliel responded with an air of nonchalance. "He has the power to alter his form at will. On that day, he became a firewall that enveloped Tartarus House and saved it from destruction."

"You created chaos and hysteria in 1823 and 1923, and again this year. The house was built in 1723. Did you work your mayhem then as well?"

"I did, although you err when calling those diversions chaos or mayhem. Trust me, you don't want to see what chaos I can cause. Every hundred years, I create confusion to keep the people from becoming complacent. Fear is a means of exerting control over the residents. This is my town, Mr. Drake, and by now the people are so afraid that they're considering abandoning it. That is profoundly satisfying to me."

"Why are you telling me these things?"

Bezaliel's voice dripped with scorn. "You fool, I'm telling you nothing. This is simply your dream."

With nothing to lose, Landry pressed on. "I escaped from Tartarus House through the portal. But I went to a place of absolute darkness. Was it Purgatory?"

Bezaliel shrugged. "Call it anything you wish. Purgatory is a human invention by those who want to suffer. You went to the place of unfulfilled ambition. My own ambition, however, will be fulfilled. I want the book."

"The book? I don't know what you mean."

He sneered, "I can read your mind. Madame Blue asked Cate for the books. One of them is irrelevant; I want the other, the one called *Secreta Aeternitatis*. You will get it for me."

"Why don't you get it yourself?"

"Madame Blue has certain powers, and she has hidden it from me. Get the book from her, bring it to the portal, and put it in the water. If you don't give it to me within twenty-four hours, someone close to you will die!" he screamed before disappearing in a cloud of blue smoke.

Landry woke when he heard the front door open and close. Simba jumped off the bed, his barks turning to yelps of joy as Cate peeked into the bedroom. "Is everything okay?" she asked.

He nodded. "Where are the books Madame Blue wanted? And what are they, anyway?"

She gave him a quizzical look. "Have you been lying here thinking about those books? They're two ancient volumes I found in a hidden recess inside that secret room. A box of magical objects too. Madame Blue explained what everything was. She's interested in a book of secrets that may enable us to stop the Harbingers."

"Did you give them to her?"

Puzzled, Cate furrowed her brows. "What's going on? How do you know about the books?"

"Where are they, Cate?"

"I gave them to her, okay? She said she can protect them from Bezaliel. What the hell is this about?"

"I had...well, another dream, I guess. But not really a dream. Something much more real that ended just before you came home. Bezaliel is going to kill one of us if I don't give him the book he wants within twenty-four hours. I believe him, Cate, and we have to do it."

She sat on the bed, and Simba jumped back up, positioning his head under her hand until she gave him a pat. "Landry, you've been through a harrowing experience. I never wanted you to set foot in that house again, and I know you didn't go willingly. I hope now you'll listen to everyone who's told you how dangerous it is.

"He gave you twenty-four hours to deliver the book. Let's get Madame Blue's advice. Call her while I pour us some wine."

The seeress listened as Landry explained what had happened, and she said, "I believe Bezaliel is creating the Harbingers. The latest one was the most tragic, but there may be worse ahead. I've looked at the book he wants, and we simply cannot allow him to have it. To those who believe the paranormal is a fantasy, what I'm about to tell you would sound ridiculous. But you, Landry—you of all people understand that what we're dealing with is all too real. This is no magic trick or sleight of hand or hocus-pocus. This is supernatural activity at its most deadly.

"In the wrong hands, the *Secrets of Eternity* book could impart unlimited power. If we give it to Bezaliel, he will hold the keys to absolute dominion over this planet and everyone on it."

CHAPTER TWENTY-SIX

Jules Beckman's head snapped up from his desk as a deep, thunderous bell pealed. Groggy, he looked around the room, got his bearings, and realized he had fallen asleep. The nearby window was open to catch the night breeze, and the deafening sound that woke him were the bells in the steeple of St. Louis Cathedral next door tolling twelve times. It was midnight.

His desk lay strewn with old books, documents, articles and newspaper clippings—everything Jules had found that included the name Bezaliel Moros. He had done considerable research earlier, but as the Harbingers continued, he believed the person with the mythical names was behind them. So he spent hours digging through documents in the archives that no one had seen for over two centuries.

Jules reread the things he already learned about Bezaliel, making notes to avoid missing some fact that might come in handy. The name shown on the land grant of 1722 was Bezaliel Moros, Greek through and through and likely a recent immigrant, although Jules located no earlier record. Plenty of foreigners had landed at the new port of

New Orleans, looking to make a fortune in the New World.

Early notes indicated Moros had been a wealthy indigo planter, but Jules found no records to prove it. Whatever the source, he was a man of means, because in 1723 he built a majestic mansion—one of the city's largest—on Dauphine Street. The house would have cost several million dollars in today's money, Jules calculated. Other entrepreneurs were building fancy homes in New Orleans then, but only one was a mystery.

Bezaliel was an odd name to hang on a kid, Jules thought as he researched the ancient Greek word. Its base meaning was "damaged," but the name itself belonged to a mythological figure—one of two hundred fallen angels called the Watchers. According to the apocryphal book of Enoch, God sent watcher angels to Earth to protect humans, but they developed a lust for its beautiful women. Some watchers seduced and impregnated them, creating a race of hybrid giants who ravaged the Earth and threatened the existence of humans.

Hybrid giants like the flesh-eating monster in the attic?

No, no, Jules assured himself. *That's too much of a stretch. Just because the man's name is Bezaliel doesn't mean he kept a hybrid giant in the attic at Tartarus House. Those words on the floor plan mean something else. I'm not sure what, but with Landry Drake's help, I intend to find out.*

Maybe the answer lies with the man who lives in the house now—the man who calls himself Proteus Moros. Is he a descendant of the original owner? Or perhaps an imposter, a squatter posing as someone else? Whoever he is, he also has the name of a very interesting Greek god.

Jules Beckman knew his Greek mythology. And thus he was aware Proteus was the god of deceit and change who had the power to see into the future. He was also a shape-shifter, able to become anything he pleased, animate or inanimate.

The hours flew by as Jules scoured pages filled with eerie illustrations and cryptic incantations. Typically calm, he became increasingly nervous, and beads of sweat formed on his brow. He had heard tales of the wrath of Bezaliel and the deceptions of Proteus, and tonight his academic curiosity had led him to a place from which there was no turning back. Overwhelmed with stress and exhaustion, he rested his head on the table for a moment, awaking when the cathedral bells chimed midnight.

There's much more to learn about these gods, but it must wait until tomorrow, Jules thought as he yawned, stretched and closed the window. He shut down his computer and shook his head at the scene of chaos on his desk. Papers were strewn about, books and manuscripts lay open, and a legal pad filled with notes bore testament to the hours he'd spent. The condition of his office was an abomination to a man obsessed with neatness and order. He walked into the dark hallway and turned to look once more. His office was a mess, and his penchants for organization and neatness almost drove him back inside.

Almost.

It must wait until tomorrow. I'm exhausted, and I can clean everything up tomorrow.

He locked his office door and took the broad marble stairs down to the lobby. Midnight was late for him, and he stifled another yawn as he waved goodnight to the security guard. His route home was a nine-block walk down Decatur, across Canal and a few blocks further along Magazine Street. He'd made the trek so many times he could do it in his sleep, but as he walked, he thought about Bezaliel and Proteus and everything he'd learned. After some time, he glanced up and saw two street signs—the intersection of St. Ann and Dauphine Streets, nowhere near his destination. In fact, he'd walked in the opposite direction.

"How on earth did I end up here?" he muttered,

thinking he should turn around and head home while instead turning the corner and walking half a block down. The streetlight on the corner provided no light here; Tartarus House loomed before him like a specter from a forgotten era. He took in the mansion's weathered and crumbling I, its three floors reaching into the dark sky, and the veil of mist twirling through the vines in the unkept front yard. The structure's dark, Gothic design and the haunting statues in the yard were somehow captivating.

The broken windows gazed out like vacant eyes, reflecting the pale light of the moon. He had heard the tales about this old house—the flickers of light passing across upstairs windows seen by so many—but tonight the decaying old mansion appeared quiet. Despite the ominous aura that enveloped the house, Jules had an inexplicable pull toward it. Some unseen force offered to satisfy his curiosity and provide revelations of age-old mysteries whose answers he sought.

A creaking sound broke the stillness of the night. Across the tangled yard, the front door swung open. Where there had been none, a faint light now emanated from inside, providing a backdrop for a petite silhouette standing in the doorway. A familiar, tender voice called to him.

"Jules! Jules, darling, is it really you?"

Oh my God! Oh my God, that voice! I haven't heard that voice in, what…twenty years?

"Celia? Is that you? How…how can…"

"Yes, Jules darling, it's me! Come here and hold me!"

He raced through the gate, tripping over the twisted undergrowth and taking a hard fall. Pulling himself up, he stumbled up the steps and saw his long-deceased wife, Celia, standing in the doorway. She was short, just five feet tall, and thin as a rail. She wore a huge smile, and as she opened her arms to welcome him, he raced across the porch to hold her once again. How this was possible—how she returned from the dead—was of no consequence. The house held mystical properties, and his wildest dream had been granted. All he wanted was to touch her face just once more. With tears streaming down his cheeks, Jules ran through the doorway, but she stepped backward, fading into the luminescence. Dazed and as giddy as a child, he followed her into a dimly lit parlor.

The door slammed shut behind him, jarring him out of the fantasy and squarely back into reality. Where he'd last seen his beloved Celia stood an imposing figure wearing a long black robe and a pointed hat.

Proteus. The shape-shifter.

Jules fell to his knees, sobbing. "That wasn't fair. That wasn't fair at all."

"Life isn't fair, Jules. I wanted to talk to you, and I conjured up the one thing that would bring you inside."

"Why? Why show her to me? You can't imagine the pain…"

"You are correct; I cannot imagine it. I lack certain emotions—feelings of love and caring and empathy simply don't exist for me. Nor does pain, which over the years has proven interesting."

Filled with more questions than fear, Jules stood and said, "I'm guessing you're Proteus Moros, and a moment ago you appeared to me as my late wife."

The man said nothing.

"How old are you?"

"Far older than you can imagine."

"Hundreds of years?"

He twisted his face into a grimace-like smile, a gesture he clearly didn't use often. "Thousands."

"Who is Bezaliel Moros to you? Your father, perhaps, even though he lived three hundred years ago?"

The being appeared annoyed. "Years are of no consequence to us. You ask too many questions, Mr. Beckman. I brought you here to ask questions of my own."

Jules felt a rush of courage even as he realized his

chances of leaving this house alive were few. If he had to die at the hand of this man, he'd at least learn what all this was about. "I'll answer your questions. But tell me who you are."

"I am who you say I am. Proteus. In this society where surnames are required, mine is Moros, the god of doom. It is the same with Bezaliel, who came before me, and it shall be the same with those who follow."

Jules shook his head. "What are you talking about? Are you a descendant of Bezaliel?"

The man threw his head back and laughed sardonically. "You can't be blamed for not understanding. You mortals have such narrow imaginations. Everything must fit precisely into a mold, or else it's impossible for you to comprehend. Well, Mr. Jules Beckman, tonight I'm going to show you things you never imagined. It will be the final and most interesting night of your miserable life."

"Why me?" he stammered as a shudder of fear swept over him. He looked about the room, wondering how he might escape. If he kept the man talking, perhaps he might have the chance to call for help. The French Quarter was just outside, after all. "Why me? I've never set foot in this house before. What have I done to you?"

"You've done nothing to me, but your mind contains a trove of historical information, and the archives where you work contain many, many more. There are papers of which you aren't aware, things that still lie hidden in that old building, ones that might create difficulties. You are dabbling in dangerous waters. You have found the paper on which Bezaliel wrote a description of the third floor of this house. Are the words true? Definitely. Is it potentially harmful to us? Enough so that you must cease your meddling at once, and tonight it will stop."

Jules recalled the words on the house plan. *The place where the flesh-eating monster lives.*

His heart pounded as he considered how to get away.

Although there was almost no chance he'd make it, he had to try. Proteus intended to make sure he stopped meddling, and Jules understood what that meant. He darted across the parlor, dodging dusty, ruined furniture to reach the door. He grabbed the knob and twisted it first one direction, then the other. He rattled, pushed and pulled, but the ancient lock held fast. He glanced back and saw Proteus standing just behind him.

"You can't leave because it's too late. Your night of reckoning has arrived."

"Let me go. I promise I'll walk away and never return. I won't tell anyone…"

"You involved Landry Drake, and that was an unforgivable error. He has already become an irritation, and he must be eliminated as well. Now come with me, Mr. Jules Beckman. I have something to show you that I promise you have never seen before."

Landry must be eliminated as well? "Where…where do you want me to go?"

"Why, to the place that you found so interesting when you saw the drawings of this house. Up to the third floor, the place where the flesh-eating monster lives."

CHAPTER TWENTY-SEVEN

Jules glanced everywhere in the parlor, searching for something…anything that might serve as a weapon. He realized the powers this man possessed, but he had to fight for his life.

"Follow me," Proteus said, turning to go into the next room. Jules instead picked up a heavy vase and moved toward one of the tall windows that opened onto the porch. He lifted the object and flung it toward the window.

In a nanosecond, Proteus raised his arm and pointed a slender wand toward the vase, stopping its progress in midair and causing it to fall harmlessly to the floor. In another circumstance, it would have been a fascinating trick, a feat of suspended animation, but in the dire situation Jules faced, it was proof that his life was almost over.

"Please don't hurt me. I'll do anything you ask."

Proteus took his arm and dragged him into a musty hallway. The ancient floorboards creaked, strips of wallpaper hung down in eerie shreds, and the air felt heavy and stagnant. Cobwebs dangled from the ceiling as they approached a rickety staircase. Proteus said, "Go up," and

Jules grasped a chipped, faded handrail worn smooth from years of use. The risers groaned as the men ascended, and Jules had a sense of sadness, as if treading upon the memories of others from long ago. Shadows danced along the walls, and the temperature plummeted, sending a chill down his spine.

The second floor—a long hallway with rooms on each side that Jules recognized from the plans—transported him to a bygone era. Long ago, an artist had created bayou scenes on the walls; as faded as they were, and as perilous his plight, Jules took in the beauty and majesty of the landscapes.

Proteus pushed Jules along to a door, which he opened to reveal another stairway, this one so steep and narrow he was forced to sidle up the stairs in an awkward fashion. Jules hesitated in the darkness, but his captor pushed and prodded him up every riser. With a final shove, Jules fell forward into the expansive room, losing his footing and collapsing to the floor. He lay shivering in a heap as shafts of moonlight through broken windowpanes revealed faded paintings and aged furniture. The air hung heavy with a potent mix of decay, lingering despair, and a sense of impending doom.

His own doom.

Alerted by a creaking noise, he turned to see the door swing shut. Proteus had left, closing the door behind him. Knowing it would be locked, Jules still tried the knob, which turned but wouldn't open.

Alone in the enormous room, he retrieved his phone, lit the flashlight, and tried to remember the floor plan. Was the stairway the only means of egress, or might a hidden exit lie behind the doors that lined the end walls? He opened one after another, finding closets packed to the brim with trunks, boxes and wooden crates. Others held racks with hangars; the coats and dresses and formal wear that once hung on them now lay in moth-eaten, disintegrating piles of cloth on the floor. One door was locked, and the last was empty except for a black square in the floor, which he recalled seeing on the floor plans for this house and Henri's building. A black square filled with dark water that shimmered in the half-light.

This is some type of portal. Henri has one too; maybe there are others, but perhaps not. What if...could I use it to escape this place?

Jules didn't know where it might take him, but facing certain death, he also didn't care. He knelt beside the square and touched its surface. The water rippled as he put his hand in and felt the bottom an inch below.

How does this thing work? He splashed the water, stirred it around, and even tried putting his foot inside, but nothing happened. Knowing his time might be running out, he gave up and returned to the ballroom.

Tall French doors led out onto the porch roof, three stories above the veranda. They would have been opened to allow in fresh air on humid midsummer evenings when the ballroom was in use, although Jules doubted if there had ever been a party here. They were sealed shut from years of neglect, and even if he broke through, there was no place to go unless he leapt off the roof to his death.

The place where the flesh-eating monster lives. Bezaliel wrote that description on the plan. And now I am trapped in that very room..

CHAPTER TWENTY-EIGHT

Jules searched the ballroom for something he could use to pick the lock. Or a key—another skeleton key hidden away in case of emergency. He found an old screwdriver and a hammer, but neither helped.

The light from his phone illuminated the surrounding area, but the far end of the cavernous room still lay in darkness. It was from there that he picked up the first alarming sound, a quiet hissing noise like steam escaping from a valve. It began, but stopped, and all was quiet again. In the gloom, he saw a tall figure, its arms outstretched. A person, or so it seemed.

"Proteus!" he cried, and the figure retreated into the darkness. Then came that hiss again, as light as a breeze yet somehow menacing, deadly. Much closer now. *Perhaps it's a snake,* he thought, but something was different about the sound. He could hear but not see the figure, and Jules took a few cautious steps backwards, thinking if he made it to one of the closets along the wall behind him, pull out a few boxes and shut himself inside, the animal—the thing, whatever it was—might not be able to reach him.

As he ambled clumsily backwards, monitoring the

gloom, he noticed movement. The thing was back, and for every step he took, it took two, until the distance between them was halved. He still hadn't reached the closet, and now he ran, throwing open the door, tossing out one box after another and only stopping when a nasty stench wafted into the closet. He turned to see the thing mere feet away, its gaping mouth filled with sharp fangs and its noxious breath almost enough to knock him out.

Jules calmed his fear. Resigned to his fate, the scholar in him studied the thing moving back and forth. He spoke words aloud, although no one would ever hear them. It was a last testament, a final description of one's own demise.

"I'm facing Proteus. He was a man earlier, but now he's transformed into an enormous arachnid that's crouching before me. In the half-light I see a face with humanoid features but the torso of a gigantic spider. Its mouth is open wide and filled with inch-long fangs. Its breath is nasty, and it slobbers. There's some kind of cloth on its back, likely the black robe Proteus wore earlier, because Proteus is my adversary. He's the Greek shape-shifter who has morphed into the flesh-eating monster in the attic."

The thought crossed Jules's mind that the only flesh available to be eaten in the attic was his own.

When the time came, it was mercifully quick. The thing leapt into the air, pounced on Jules, and tore out his throat with one mighty bite from its jagged teeth. Soon all that remained was a pile of clothing lying in a heap on the floor.

CHAPTER TWENTY-NINE

The next morning when Jules failed to meet Henri at Café du Monde, Henri called his phone but got voicemail. Knowing how out of character it was for Jules to miss an appointment without notice, Henri walked across Jackson Square to the Cabildo and spoke to the security guard, who checked a log and said Jules had left at midnight—very late for him—and hadn't come in today. Since he was always among the first to show in the morning, the guard had become worried. He added, "Jules is such a nice guy. I sure hope nothing's happened to him."

At Henri's request, the guard called Jules's assistant. After Henri introduced himself and explained his connection to Jules, the young man admitted he was worried too. "He's never been this late before," the young man said. Henri asked what Jules had been working on and what he might have left on his desk when he'd departed the building last night.

The assistant replied, "That also concerns me. It's stacked high with books and manuscripts, and Jules never goes home leaving things a mess. I mean *never*. About what he was working on, I noticed a yellow pad filled with notes. It appears he was looking for references to the names Bezaliel and Proteus Moros. Greek gods, maybe?"

"May I take a look?" Henri asked, and the young clerk escorted him upstairs, allowing Henri to rummage through the stacks of research materials piled upon the desk. There was no mistaking what Jules was after—he had scribbled the Moros name repeatedly, drawing arrows from Bezaliel to Proteus. Under the former name he had listed bullet points: *indigo planter???; name means "damaged"; one of the Watchers; fallen angel; race of hybrid giants who rebelled against God.* Under Proteus's name he wrote *god of deceit and change* and highlighted the words *shape-shifter* with a yellow marker.

As he left the Cabildo, Henri decided to look at the house he hadn't yet seen. He called Landry, assuming he would want to come along. But once he learned Jules was missing, Landry insisted he stay away from that block of Dauphine Street.

He said, "Don't do it, Henri. There's something ominous about that place, something as bad as anything I've seen in my career. I might have died in there, Henri. Thank God I returned through the portal. You have no business going near that place, especially alone. If that's where Jules went last night, then we should call the police. Before they go inside, I'll explain what happened to me. They may not believe it, but at least they'll be forewarned. I have an awful feeling about Jules. I think the first place they should look for him is on the third floor, and there's no telling what they'll find. I like him, and I hope he's okay, but like I said, if he went inside, there's no telling what happened."

Cate listened from just outside Landry's office. She found it interesting that she had warned Landry about going back, but he continued to profess an interest in doing so. Now he was warning Henri not to go. She stepped in and said, "Couldn't help but overhear. Can you put Henri on speaker?"

Henri was saying, "Jules told me the officers have been there before, and I don't know if they'll do it again. We have no proof Jules went there, and I wouldn't be surprised if they explain that they're a little busy right now, what with the Harbingers killing people and all."

"I'll call Shane Young. I'm certain he'll help. Henri, come back to the office."

"Don't order me around!" he said, half jesting. "You're beginning to sound like Cate."

She snorted. "Would you rather we just let you go off and do crazy things like Landry does?"

"Enough bashing!" Landry declared. "I'm hanging up now. See you back here, Henri."

A New Orleans police detective not much older than Landry, Shane Young had been involved with several of Landry's unusual cases that became episodes on the Paranormal Network. He'd played a role in a bizarre story Landry called "The Experiments," and Landry had enlisted his help in several since.

Detective Young was always ready to listen because he had seen enough to believe in the supernatural. No matter how farfetched a story Landry spun, Shane Young would accept it because he respected Landry and his work. That came in handy because Landry was able to skip the convincing part. Instead of a skeptical officer rolling his eyes as Landry talked, he had a sympathetic ear and someone who understood there were things that defied explanation.

Shane listened, said he'd contact the cops who had been to Tartarus House earlier, and get back as quickly as he could. Within ninety minutes he called, saying, "Meet me at the house, and find out if Jack Blair can come too. He rescued that girl trapped inside, and maybe he can help us."

Jack was excited and agreed to meet Landry at the house, and Landry told Phil to be ready to go in fifteen minutes. Henri opted to stay at the office but suggested they include Madame Blue, who had worked with Detective Young in the past and whose extrasensory powers might come in handy. She agreed to join them.

Landry turned to Cate. "Mother, may I go to the scary haunted house now that the nice detective with the gun is going to be there with me?"

Cate laughed aloud, then gave him a warning. "Guns won't stop supernatural creatures and you know it. I like the idea of several people going, but please watch your step, Landry. Don't get out of Shane's sight. Promise?"

As he crossed his heart and gave a sly smile, Cate saw crossed fingers on his other hand. She threw up her hands, shook her head, and walked back to her office.

CHAPTER THIRTY

The group assembled one by one outside the old mansion. Landry's friend Shane Young came alone after conferring with the sergeant who had been inside Tartarus House earlier. The older cop, who couldn't have known Shane believed in the paranormal, assured Shane he saw nothing out of the ordinary in the house. "Just a bunch of magic stuff and potions and the like," he explained. "The place is a dump, and I saw nothing to indicate people lived there." He refused to come along, saying it was a waste of time and he had better things to do.

"You could read his body language a mile away," Shane said to Landry. "He's afraid of that place. He experienced something himself." The detective also thought it better that other cops hadn't come along. They had five people already, and that should be enough firepower to deal with whatever they encountered. Their goal was to find Jules Beckman, and too many people on the scene might make that mission more difficult.

Jack called Landry aside and asked if he minded sharing whatever story came out of their adventure today. The two were close friends and had investigated a lot of paranormal events together, but Landry laughed at his question.

"Seriously, Jack? I love you, buddy, but it's my story. I'm the one doing the inviting. You're along for the ride."

"Okay, but if paranormal stuff happens, will you share footage I can pass on to my newsroom? No documentary until you've done one—I understand you have dibs on that—but if we uncover something interesting, I'd like to have a news exclusive." That was fine with Landry since his cable network didn't provide current, "breaking news" stories. Instead, his *Bayou Hauntings* and *Mysterious America* series comprised two-hour episodes aired across the nation.

Detective Young asked Landry if the house was occupied. He smiled and replied, "*Occupied* may not be quite the right word," explaining that Angie Bovida believed a woman kidnapped her, while Landry had been ejected from the property by a man wearing a long cape. But that didn't mean either of them was alive. Or human.

Bezaliel Moros held title to the property and had since he built the house in 1723. Clearly he was long deceased. Perhaps, depending on what he really was. Then there was the man—or something—Landry had seen on his last visit, who also said his name was Moros. A relative, perhaps? An impostor who was as much an intruder as they? An apparition who didn't exist, or something worse?

"In a nutshell," Landry concluded, "from all the information Jules Beckman, Henri and I have found, I'd say 'people' aren't 'living there.' Bezaliel and Proteus aren't human. Madame Blue, do you agree?"

She shrugged. "What does it matter? Each of us will be trespassing into their realm, no matter who or what they are. Or perhaps they won't be there at all. Now leave me be. I must prepare myself." She walked away from the others and stood in silence, taking in the mansion from top to bottom, observing every broken pane and rotted post, every grotesque, ruined statue in the yard, all while inhaling deeply, drawing in the very essence of the structure they were about to enter.

After some time meditating, Madame Blue asked Detective Young if he knew the house's reputation for being one of the city's most haunted, adding, "I've been inside twice, and I experienced supernatural events both times. Landry's visit was far worse; there's a paranormal portal on the third floor, which is described on old house plans as the place where a flesh-eating monster lives. He can tell you about that later. Now I am ready to go inside."

Although the mansion looked as dark and empty as ever, Landry was prepared to confront whomever they met. Just before they passed through the rickety gate, Madame Blue said, "Our mission is to find Jules Beckman, but I cannot caution you enough about the dangers within these walls. Someone may get hurt...or worse." She turned and led them into the garden.

"It's her standard caveat," Landry whispered to the others as they filed in one by one. "She's being paid by our network, and she's limiting her liability. She's right, though. Jules said the same thing about this place. It's the spookiest house in town."

Phil shrugged and said it was just another job for him. Jack said he was looking forward to finding out what secrets the house held.

Crossing the yard, Phil snagged his pants on the thorny vines, resulting in a string of expletives. Madame Blue shot him a harsh stare and snapped, "No more of those words! Show respect."

Phil nodded sheepishly as they climbed the stairs to the veranda, and he switched on his shoulder camera.

"It'll be locked," Landry said, reaching for the knob. "I had to use the back door last time." A few steps behind him, Madame Blue pointed a finger at the lock. "Hey, it works!" Landry said, turning it and letting the door swing open.

Phil noticed what she'd done and looked her way. Ignoring him, she eased Landry aside and declared she would enter first. Detective Young followed, his hand resting lightly on the service revolver hanging from his belt.

The parlor appeared the same as last time, except for a chilling breeze that sent shivers down Landry's spine. The others felt it too; outdoors, it was warm, but here the sudden, frigid burst of air surprised everyone except the clairvoyant, who asked them to wait in the entryway while she surveyed the musty room. The air felt thick with unseen energy, and Madame Blue whispered, "We have crossed the threshold that connects us with the restless spirits of the past. This house holds much sadness, much despair, and much horror."

She raised her voice. "Speak to us, dear ones. Reveal your feelings, your pain, and your sadness." She instructed the others to come to the middle of the room, form a circle, and hold hands. Everyone but Phil joined the circle; he panned the camera on the group and around the room as Landry told them what he knew about Bezaliel Moros, the supposed indigo planter who built the mansion. He stopped when Madame Blue held up a finger and murmured, "Shh! Listen!"

There were faint whispers—a chorus of voices both distant and unmistakable. As they grew louder and clearer, Madame Blue murmured, "The children," and the others understood they were hearing the haunting echoes of boys and girls whose spirits were trapped inside this house. The sounds became more distinct; there were snippets of conversations, laughter, and playful games of children who died long, long ago. The ghostly chatter evoked both a sense of innocence and utter sorrow, a reminder of the tragedies that had occurred on this spot.

"Come play with us." The invitation wafted through the

air like mournful music on a breeze, a plaintive plea for companionship from another world. "Follow me," Madame Blue said, leading them through a doorway into the dining room. "They're in here."

"How many are there?" Landry asked as the clairvoyant relegated them to a corner.

She answered, "Too many to count."

"What happened to them?"

She put a finger to her lips and whispered, "No sudden movements. No cries or loud noises. Just stay quiet and watch." She spoke aloud to the empty room. "Where are you, boys and girls? We are your friends. Show yourselves to us."

Madame Blue pointed to a corner where an old playpen gradually materialized, remnants of toys scattered about inside it and on the floor. Landry glanced at Phil, who gave a thumbs-up. The camera was capturing everything. "They may speak telepathically in my mind," the seeress advised. "Or they may speak aloud. Different strokes for different ghosts." Landry raised his eyebrows; it was the first attempt at humor he'd heard from her.

Dust motes floated in the thick air as the dim light filtered through tattered curtains. Landry's heart raced as he looked around the large room. In each chair around the dusty dining table was the ethereal presence of a ghostly child. They wore faded, tattered hospital gowns; some appeared healthy while others bore visible signs of ailments and surgeries that took their lives long ago.

Other children wearing gowns, younger than the ones at the table, sat in the playpen, laughing and playing. One's arm was in a cast; another had only one foot, the other having been removed below the knee. *We're intruders in their world*, Landry thought as he and his friends watched the interaction, the innocent merriment and laughter and pain as the feelings of these ghosts mingled with their own senses. A wave of emotions washed over him—empathy, sadness and…fear. He saw Phil wipe away a tear. Jack appeared overcome with feelings as well, but Madame Blue stood stoically and spoke to the children as calmly as if she were conversing with someone over lunch. Shane Young stood to one side and looked about the room, prepared to respond in case something happened.

"Why are you in this house, dear ones?" she asked, and a wispy figure, a girl perhaps ten years old, floated to her side.

"Because we have no parents. We are orphans, and we have nowhere else to go."

"What year is it, child?" The waif gave her a blank look and shrugged, and the seeress took another tack. "What happened to your mother and father?"

"They died when the *St. James* blew up."

"The *St. James*? Was that a building?"

"No, ma'am. The *St. James* was a steamboat. It exploded out on the lake a few months ago, and my uncle brought me here because they couldn't afford to keep me."

Madame Blue glanced at Landry, who was tapping his iPhone. A moment later he said, "She's referring to an actual event. A number of people died on Lake Pontchartrain when the boilers of the steamboat *St. James* exploded."

"When?" Jack asked. "This little girl said it was a few months ago. That can't be right."

Madame Blue explained, "To her it is. In her world, she hasn't been here that long. These children are trapped in time. When did that explosion take place, Landry?"

"It happened on the fifth of July, 1852."

CHAPTER THIRTY-ONE

It saddened them to realize that these children were trapped in a time and place almost two hundred years in the past. As time passed and the world changed, they remained imprisoned in an otherworldly dimension.

"Why do most look so emaciated?" Jack asked. "And why are so many maimed and diseased?"

"This was an orphanage where they should have been cared for and attended to, but all they received were the bare necessities. No love, no concern, no tears if one died, or if they all did." Madame Blue reached to pat a toddler's head but watched her hand pass through the apparition like mist. "We must release them and give them peace."

As she spoke, the laughter and voices grew fainter, and the room darkened as a thick blanket of clouds obscured rays of sunlight that had peeked through the gritty windowpanes. Something changed; the spectral children felt it, hugging each other, older ones gathering the young close as fear clouded their faces. They backed away from a dark corner and cowered.

There a figure materialized in the darkness—one whom Landry recognized. "Ah, the root of the problem. Proteus

Moros," the seeress sneered as the children drew back in terror. "Why have you not released these pathetic little ones? Does tormenting their souls give you pleasure?"

"Silence!" he roared, and the horrified children vanished in a flash. He pointed a bony finger at Landry and screamed, "This man has trespassed before, and now he brings you here. Get out, all of you. Get out before you anger me!"

Detective Young stepped forward, unsure of what he was getting himself into, and drew his pistol.

"Take us to the ballroom," Landry said.

"You've been there. You used the portal."

"Take us. I want to find out if Jules Beckman is there."

"Madame Blue, advise Mr. Drake how dangerous his demand is," Proteus said. "You at least have an inkling of the power and mystery of this house and the grounds upon which it was built. Mr. Drake should know too; he experienced it himself. Will you allow him to put the lives of everyone here, including yourself, in peril?"

The seeress took a defiant step toward him. "What do you want, Proteus? Why do you continue this battle? You have inhabited this mansion for ages. You understand the secrets of the house and the grounds, but is this how you want to spend the rest of your days? We can free these children, we can solve the mysteries, and we can release your tormented soul in the process. Where you would go next, I dare not predict. But is the hell you face better than this hell on earth, roaming the halls of the prison your father, Bezaliel, created for you?"

Proteus's reaction was instant and filled with fury. With a roar, he pointed the wand he held at her, but Madame Blue casually raised her hand palm out and laughed.

"Simple magic won't work on me. I know far more spells than you. You may be a fearsome creature with many powers, a being who can strike fear into the hearts of mortals, but you know little about magic, and you're wasting your time with me. Now allow Landry to go to the ballroom."

The cop drew his pistol more for his own peace of mind than any thought it might be effective against this being who he understood was human in appearance only.

But in a flash it was over, as Proteus disappeared in a pillar of white smoke.

Landry looked at the others. "Are we all okay?" he asked, then realized they were missing someone. Jack wasn't in the room. No one saw him leave, and when Landry shouted his name, they heard no reply. With Shane at his side, he ran from room to downstairs room, searching for his missing friend. He texted but got no response, and he edged around Madame Blue, who stood at the bottom of the stairway with her fingers pressed hard to her temples and started upstairs. Phil grabbed his camera and ran after Landry and the detective, but Landry sent both back, saying he had to do this alone.

"No, Landry!" the psychic shouted. "I sense Jack is in the ballroom, but it's too risky for you to go!"

"Is Jack all right? Can you see him in your mind?"

She nodded. "He put himself in grave danger by going there, but Proteus will not harm him. Bezaliel wants the book, and they are using Jack as bait."

"Then I have to go!"

"I'll go with you," the cop said, but again Landry told him to stay put. Madame Blue said, "Landry, you're placing yourself in great danger. I managed to deflect his magic, and you saw only an inkling of his power when you were in the house earlier. It's too risky to go there now. You cannot imagine what mayhem he's capable of."

Disregarding her warning, he raced up the stairs, ran down the hallway, and opened the door he had seen in a dream. Before him lay the narrow, unlit stairwell. He scrambled up, each wooden step creaking and groaning under his hurried footsteps. When he reached the door at the top, a mixture of fear and determination coursed through his veins, and his heart pounded in his chest.

Landry put his ear to the door but heard nothing. He tried the knob; it turned easily, and to his surprise, this time nothing on the other side blocked the door. It swung back to reveal the lofty ballroom where he'd been held captive by the spider creature. He drew back in surprise and looked around; the room was different; it resembled nothing he'd encountered in his paranormal career.

It had transformed into a twisted, nightmarish realm with walls adorned with grotesque symbols that glowed with energy. The air was stifling—hot and milky-thick with an oppressive stench that enveloped Landry like a suffocating shroud. At the opposite end of the room, a swirling mass of shadows and malevolence rose halfway to the ceiling. Half-hidden in its midst was something large and dark and feral—the frightening beast he'd encountered earlier.

The malodorous, spiderlike creature sidled out of the mist on eight spindly legs that supported its bulbous torso. As it drew closer, Landry saw its face resembled that of a human, but it had beady eyes that glowed a steady red and a grotesque mouth that reached from ear to ear and contained a hundred spiny teeth.

Trembling, Landry held his ground, and the beast stopped twenty feet away. It spoke telepathically, its taunting words slithering into Landry's mind.

You are an impertinent fool who acts without thinking. You want answers. You want to find your friend and the man from the museum. You want everything at once and without consequence. Your flawed audacity has failed you this time. You freed yourself from me once before, and now what you want shall be revealed, but the price is the forfeit of your life.

Remembering Madame Blue's cautionary words and realizing he had underestimated the power of the shape-shifter Proteus, Landry glanced toward the open doorway, but he watched the door slowly shut. The room seemed to contort as the walls closed in around him. Desperation clawed at Landry's heart; was this how his life would end?

Why did I come searching for Jack and Jules without preparing?

Are you afraid, Mr. Drake? Is the very sight of me too much for you to bear? Have you made a fatal error?

The words echoed in his mind as the creature moved closer. Landry took a step back, tripping over something behind him. He fell awkwardly to the floor amidst a pile of clothing that he'd tripped over, and he saw something that revealed an awful truth. In the dust lay Jules's plaid golf cap, and Landry realized Henri's friend was dead, but perhaps there was hope for Jack.

"Where is Jack?" Landry cried as the spiderlike thing raised itself on its front two legs and opened its jaws. Its teeth glistened, and its breath was noxious; Landry ducked his head, waiting for what was to come, but suddenly it drew back, curled its hairy legs beneath its torso, and scurried to the far end of the ballroom. Landry turned to see Madame Blue standing in the now-open doorway, her hands in the air and her fingers pointed at the beast. Her lips moved, but Landry could hear no sound. Her eyes were closed as if she were in a state of suspended animation, but when the beast retreated, she dropped her arms, took a deep breath, and said, "Come, Landry. You must leave this place now!"

"No! I have to find Jack!"

"I sense he is in no danger for now, but you are. Come with me!"

CHAPTER THIRTY-TWO

In the front parlor, an increasingly belligerent Landry confronted Madame Blue. His voice trembled with urgency as he demanded answers. "There's a pile of clothes on the floor up there," he said. "And a golf cap. Jules Beckman's golf cap. That thing killed him, and it would have killed me too. Jack is next, and we must save him."

The enigmatic psychic met Landry's agitation with serene composure. Her wisdom transcended the mortal realm, and she told him, "Jack is on the top floor, and he's alive. That's all I can say. Perhaps Proteus locked him in one of the closets; regardless, he won't be harmed. It's you they want, and despite what I accomplished upstairs, my powers are limited against him. It's fortunate I could free you this time, but I cannot promise anything if you insist on challenging him again."

Landry burned with a fierce determination. He couldn't bear to stand idly by while Jack's life was at stake. "I'm going back up there to free Jack. I have no choice."

"Yes, you do. You can lure Proteus out of the ballroom. Bring him down here, and one of us can go look for Jack."

Detective Young, the pragmatic one in a sea of

supernatural confrontations, nodded. "I'll go."

But the question remained—how could they lure the malevolent entity Proteus downstairs when he possessed such powers? Madame Blue offered an idea. "It may trade one problem for another, but my sources in the spirit realm say the way to entice him here is to anger him. Phil, turn on your camera. I'm going to summon the children."

They gathered around the seeress as she stood in the center of the room, her arms outstretched. "Little ones, come to us. Tell us how we might help you," she beckoned in a soothing, gentle voice.

They watched in fascination as spirits appeared here and there about the room. One girl held a doll, a boy had a spinning top, and others clutched their own favorites. Three girls manifested in the middle of a game of jump rope. Although these were trapped entities and lost souls, they also were children, and their innocence was both refreshing and sad to behold.

"Will someone speak to us?" Madame Blue said in a soothing voice. "We want to help you. Which of you will speak to me?"

Hesitant for only a moment, one by one the figures swept across the room, swirling around the psychic and communicating telepathically, implanting their words directly into her mind. She listened in solemn silence before turning to Phil and Landry.

"He holds their souls captive. Until he releases them, the children are trapped here."

"Proteus?"

"They don't know him by name, but they tell me it's a different entity than the one we saw earlier. That frightens me because it means both members of the Moros family are in this house. I had hoped that wasn't the case. Two supernatural beings, father and son, Bezaliel and Proteus. And it's Bezaliel, the more formidable one, who holds the children captive."

She raised her hands and cried out, "Bezaliel, I command you to appear!"

"You're wasting your time." Contemptuous words rang in the air, and they turned as one to see Proteus standing by the fireplace. "You can summon Bezaliel, but he will not respond unless he chooses. His power far surpasses your own, woman. Get out of our house!"

"You killed Jules Beckman!" Landry shouted. "We will leave, but only when you release Jack, and Bezaliel frees the children."

The mocking laugh echoed throughout the room. "You mortal fool! I can free your friend with a nod of my head, but Bezaliel will never agree to your demands! He wants the book. Do you want your friend back? I will give him to you. Done!" He raised his wand, pointed it at a rotting sofa, and whispered something. Seconds later, Jack appeared, lying on the couch and staring up at them blankly.

"Jack! Are you okay?" As Phil's camera rolled on, Landry ran to his side, where his friend said he was okay but groggy.

Proteus bellowed, "I have done as you asked. I delivered your friend. Now give Bezaliel the book!"

"Summon your father," Landry said.

Black smoke erupted around Proteus, and his eyes flashed in fury. "No!" he screamed. "Stop calling him that!"

Madame Blue said, "Like father, like son. As much as you may detest each other, there can be no denying he's your sire. You should be thankful you fared better than many of your siblings. Hybrid giants, as I believe the ancient writers described them. You may be uncommonly tall, but you're no giant. And he imbued you with the powers of the god Proteus, the shape-shifter, making you able to transform yourself into grotesque creatures like the one in the attic. Now summon Bezaliel, and we will leave."

"Never! Your friend died because you refuse to hand

over the book. I gave you back this man, but you still refuse. Our patience is wearing thin, Landry Drake! Bring Bezaliel the book!" His voice reached a crescendo, rattling the windowpanes and sending dust motes swirling about the room. He wrapped his robe around his body, raised his wand above his head, and disappeared.

CHAPTER THIRTY-THREE

The parlor fell silent, and Madame Blue declared that nothing more would be accomplished today. It was time to leave. Detective Young told Landry he'd call in a forensic team to examine Jules's clothing and look for clues. No one doubted he was dead, and a thorough search of the entire house would take place, but nothing of value would turn up. Jules Beckman's name would be added to the missing persons list.

At the front door, the seeress addressed the empty room. "Dear ones, I promise we will come back to help you. Please don't despair, children. As soon as we can, we will set you free." Ignoring the faint whispers that wafted through the room, she led the others out through the tangled yard to the sidewalk, where she turned and left them without another word.

The moment he reached the sidewalk, Landry's iPhone pinged over and over. "Looks like it stopped working when we went inside," he told Phil and Jack. They discovered the same thing had happened to their phones.

Several texts and calls had been from Cate and Henri, each unread message and failed call causing them more anxiety. Landry sent a brief text advising his phone had been without service, they were no longer inside the house, they had Jack, and they'd be at the office shortly.

Instead of returning to Channel Nine, Jack accompanied them because he needed advice. He was part of the latest Harbinger—his own kidnapping by an evil spirit. It would be the lead story on the six o'clock news, but before he could tell his boss what happened, he wanted to discuss the consequences with Landry.

With Mardi Gras fast approaching, this story might add fuel to the fears that were scaring off tourists and locals alike. Moreover, it might attract the curious to Dauphine Street, and if the foolish dared go inside the house, someone could die. Everything about Jack's experience had to be considered before he returned to his office.

As they strolled through the historic French Quarter, Jack asked what Landry knew about Madame Blue and her mystical powers. But Landry gave a shake of his head and replied, "Let's save that conversation for when we're back at the network. Henri knows more about her than I, but there's a lot we have to discuss. I want to hear everything about your disappearance, for instance."

"I'll tell you what I can, but I don't know much."

The rest of their walk was in silence as Landry's mind buzzed with questions. Back at the studio, he hoped to piece together the fragments of their otherworldly encounters, to learn more about the mysteries of Madame Blue's power over Bezaliel and Proteus, and to uncover the truth behind Jack's vanishing act.

Landry, Jack, Henri and Cate assembled in the conference room while Phil went upstairs to work on the footage he'd recorded, promising he'd return with edited material soon. Landry took a seat next to Henri, put a hand on his good friend's arm, and said, "I'm sorry to have to tell you this, but I'm certain Jules is dead." He described tripping over the pile of clothing and seeing Jules's signature golf cap. As he spoke, tears welled up in Henri's eyes, and he took a silk handkerchief from his pocket to dab at them.

"He and I were close friends, and I can count on one hand how many of those I have," Henri mused, staring into space. "There were many great conversations about his fascinating work at the Cabildo. I'll miss Jules very much."

Henri broke free from his reverie and looked at Landry. "Is it possible that he's hiding somewhere in the house or being held captive? Is there even a remote chance?"

Landry shook his head and said he believed the creature that had ensnared him, a manifestation of the shape-shifting Proteus Moros, was also the thing that killed Jules. He said Detective Young was calling in a forensics team, but Landry doubted they would find anything. This was the work of what Bezaliel described as the flesh-eating monster.

When Landry asked Jack to explain his disappearance, his recollections remained fragmented. He had wandered into the dining room and heard a noise echoing from the nearby hallway, the muffled sound of someone crying. Curious, he took the stairs to the second floor, where the sound became more distinct.

"Who's there?" he had called out, but there was no answer. Now the cries seemed to come from the top floor of the old mansion. He walked the long hallway, looking for another staircase, and as he passed a door, it swung open, revealing the same narrow risers Landry had ascended. Heedless of his safety, he began a surreal ascent, bathed in an eerie, hazy light that pierced the darkness in the stairwell, emanating from a crack at the bottom of a closed door at the top of the stairs.

He recalled reaching the door and turning the knob, but beyond that point, Jack's memories were a blank canvas. The next thing he remembered was regaining consciousness sprawled upon the tattered sofa in the parlor, where he watched Proteus bellow about wanting some book and threatening Landry before disappearing.

Footsteps pounding on the stairs interrupted their discussion. The three-hundred-year-old building carried sound well, which had necessitated the top floor being outfitted with sound-baffling insulation when it was converted to a recording and production studio. It was Phil who bounded down the stairs, and he was more excited than Landry had ever seen him. He raced to the conference room, placed his laptop on the table, and fired it up.

In a rare exhibit of exuberance, Phil seemed like a kid on Christmas morning. "Just wait. Just wait," he mumbled over and over as he connected a cable that would allow him to display video on the eighty-five-inch flat-screen TV hanging on the far wall. He dimmed the lights, hit a button, and the playback commenced, beginning with their entering the mansion through the front door, and ending thirty-two minutes later when they left.

"I recorded the ghosts," Phil said, as that part of the video appeared on the screen. "I didn't think it'd happen."

It pleased Landry to see the children—the pitiful, lost souls who despite their plight played like the youths they were. Sometimes their tinkly, airy voices came across as faint whispers, but other times their lips moved silently as they spoke to Madame Blue telepathically.

The sight of the pitiful orphans had a profound effect on Cate. The ghostly children's faces filled her mind and tore at her heart, and she became determined to learn the mysteries behind the spectral figures in the old mansion.

As the footage progressed, Landry interrupted from time to time to interject thoughts, questions or ideas about what they were seeing. "We couldn't have done this without Madame Blue," Landry told Henri after the recording ended. "She knew what was happening in that house and about Proteus and Bezaliel. She knew Proteus wouldn't hurt Jack because it's me they're both after, and

174

she stood up to him."

"Tell me more about Madame Blue's powers," Jack said, and Henri replied she was a mysterious figure whom he had consulted for years in his role as founder and president of the Louisiana Society for the Paranormal.

"She's a legend in this city, and I can attest to her extraordinary psychic and occult abilities. In a town filled with fakes and scammers and cheats, she stands alone as the real thing. I've asked about her past, but she refuses to disclose anything. Some say she was born with her gifts, while others believe she acquired them through studying arcane texts. There are stories about her being raised by magicians in a centuries-old mansion somewhere in the South, but whatever the truth is, she can communicate with spirits to gain insights into unsolved mysteries.

"She has assisted the police several times, using her secret powers and mystical incantations to lead them in the right direction. She values her privacy, but she has grown to respect Landry and, dare I say it, myself over time, and it is my opinion that the mystery of the Harbingers will not be solved without her help."

They finished, and as he prepared to leave, Jack once again raised the question of Landry's sharing the video. When he'd asked earlier, they hadn't yet gone inside Tartarus House. Jack had hoped for some kind of paranormal experience—a poltergeist or an eerie wail or a hidden room. What had happened instead was more than any of them could have imagined, and it was far from over. Madame Blue had pledged to free the spirits of the ghostly children, and something had to be done to stop the Moros family, father and son.

Jack hoped to use the footage to further his career at Channel Nine, while understanding that it likely would become the next episode in Landry's *Bayou Hauntings* series. "Don't worry. I'll share everything with you once it's over," Landry promised. "We can't let all this become public yet. If people think the Harbingers are being orchestrated by two otherworldly beings, and if we don't have answers on how to stop them, we'll have mass hysteria."

Amid all they'd faced, Landry could not have fathomed that these initial, foreboding Harbingers were indeed the ominous preludes to a terrifying firestorm of events that lay ready to unfurl over the next few days, relentlessly intensifying as the countdown to Mardi Gras day continued.

Much like the surging floodwaters of Hurricane Katrina, the eerie Harbingers inundated New Orleans, casting a deepening shadow of dread into the hearts and minds of the city's inhabitants. All they wanted was to partake in the revelry of Carnival as they had done for generations, but as the days and nights passed, fear gripped the populace like a sinister nightmare. Every new event served as a stark reminder that the forces of darkness were in control of their city, encroaching upon their cherished traditions, shattering any semblance of normalcy and plunging them into a haunting nightmare it seemed might never end.

CHAPTER THIRTY-FOUR

The next morning Landry and Cate again brought Simba to work with them. It was becoming routine, because neither wanted to leave him alone in the apartment. He was outgoing and friendly, and he needed to be with people, not locked in a crate for hours. If the film crew wasn't shooting footage, their little boy was welcome, and his occasional curious barks and whines didn't interrupt the projects underway at the network.

When they arrived, the dog trotted into the break room, got a drink of water from a bowl on the floor, and settled down in a dog bed on the floor beside Cate's desk, happy to be part of the action and not at home by himself. Henri was on the phone, and in a moment he called to Landry, advising Madame Blue would be coming in half an hour. She wanted to talk about the Dauphine Street house and to offer a theory about the Harbingers.

They met with her in the conference room. Landry asked if she wanted to see the footage Phil had recorded, but she declined, explaining, "I'm blessed, or perhaps cursed, with a photographic memory. I don't need audio or video to jog my recollections."

"Before we get into other things, may I ask about the children?" Henri asked. "Several sources reveal the house became an orphanage, but after seeing those phantom children in the video, it's enough to break one's heart."

You're right, Cate thought. *It's also enough to make you go back and do something about it.*

Madame Blue said, "The mansion was an orphanage for most of the eighteen hundreds. The children came from various places; Confederate fathers went off to war and died, families moved away after the fall of New Orleans in 1862, and some children were left with relatives who decided they couldn't or wouldn't care for them. When McJunkin set up his office on the ground floor during the war, he let the orphans stay on the upper floors.

"Over the years, most kids who lived at Tartarus House were mistreated and abused, and most died there. Legend has it that many were buried in shallow graves in the backyard, although to my knowledge, no one has ever investigated that claim. Few children ever left during their brief lives, and the spirits of those who didn't leave remain today, waiting after all these years for release from their captivity."

Cate had remained quiet throughout the discussion. When the psychic finished, she spoke quietly. "I'm going to Tartarus House. I'm aware of the dangers—God knows we've seen what can happen there—but I can't get the children out of my mind since watching the video yesterday. There must be something we can do to free their spirits. At least I have to try."

Madame Blue nodded. "I understand your concern, and their plight saddens me deeply as well. But powerful spells keep them bound to the house. I doubt they can be freed while Bezaliel walks this earth. As tragic as the situation seems to we mortals, they are in no pain or danger. The imminent peril is the Harbingers, and in the remaining time I have this morning, we must discuss them. I'm certain that the Moros *père et fils* are behind them, and Tartarus House is their base of operations for causing the mayhem and death."

Henri agreed and asked her to elaborate on her beliefs.

"Some clues were obvious, such as the mysterious extra float that somehow appeared at the end of the Alla parade last Friday. The single black float bore a masked, robed man, silent riders, and a sign reading, 'Krewe of Moros – The Harbinger of Doom.' After examining the figure in the news coverage, I'm convinced the masked man on the float was Proteus Moros.

"Next, I reviewed the eyewitness descriptions and determined that Proteus was also the magician who disappeared in the Bourbon Street bar, in what we would later learn was the first of the Harbingers. As a shape-shifter, I think he also was the woman who kidnapped Angie Bovida inside Tartarus House. Although I could be wrong, it's my theory he's been part of every mysterious event except one.

"In my opinion, it wasn't Proteus who murdered guests at the Mardi Gras party two days ago. A robed, masked figure was the perpetrator, but I believe this time it was his father, Bezaliel, having a turn at the action. That event was by far the most gruesome of the Harbingers, and from what I have learned about the two, it's more Bezaliel's style. That might have been Proteus too, God knows he has taken countless human lives over the millennia, but my bet is that the father orchestrated the most grisly one."

Her depth of knowledge impressed Landry. "You know a great deal about the Moros family. I noticed you seemed to have a familiarity with Proteus when you confronted him, as if that wasn't your first encounter with him."

"I've dealt with them both. They're formidable opponents, and they've been able to carry on unrestrained for an unimaginably long time. It is up to us to stop them and free the spirits of the children, and I'm in the early stages of a plan that might accomplish both things. I'm not sure if it will work, and it will be risky, but we must act quickly. Mardi Gras is in four days, and I'm convinced that the supernatural events we've seen so far are simply preludes to what Bezaliel Moros intends to do on Fat Tuesday itself. He's building to a massive climax. There will be over a million people on Canal Street and in the Quarter to watch the parades, and I fear the carnage will be devastating. When my plan is complete, we must act quickly, so be prepared to move on a moment's notice."

She stood and motioned for Cate to walk her to the door. Madame Blue touched her arm and said, "You must follow your heart, my dear, but the risks are enormous, especially to Landry. Go to the house if you must, but don't take him with you. Not this time. When my plan is complete, it will require all of us to be there and stand united against these beings. Until then, he must not set foot on that property."

She left Cate standing by the door, formulating a plan of her own.

CHAPTER THIRTY-FIVE

Cate couldn't remember ever telling Landry a lie, even a little white one. In the years they'd been together, he'd been the one to sneak off on adventures she warned him about, and he was suitably chastened each time she was proven right about the dangers involved.

After Madame Blue left the office, Cate waited a few minutes before telling Landry she had received a call from an old friend from Galveston who wanted to meet for lunch. "I'm not sure how long we'll be," she added. "I've known her since high school, and we have a lot of catching up to do."

Upstairs in the production studio, Phil told his director he needed to take his pickup to the dealership and check out a problem. He'd be gone a while, but he'd have his phone. Phil picked up his video camera and walked out.

Inside Tartarus House, Cate told Phil she wanted to see the room where the children had appeared. She had watched them on the video and prayed they'd show themselves now. He took her to the dining room.

"Speak to us," she said in a quiet voice, mimicking the words Madame Blue had used to bring them out. "Show yourselves, children. I've come to talk to you."

It thrilled her when the figures appeared one by one, indistinct and hazy at first, then morphing into shadowy children in tattered clothing. A few laughed and played while some carried a burden of sadness and oppression.

Three little girls, perhaps nine or ten years old, encircled her. "Mommy!" one cried, but another said, "Shush, silly. We don't have mommies."

"My name's Cate. Who are you all?"

"I'm Marnie," the tallest girl said. "This here is Prissy, and that's Elva. Those ain't our real names, just ones we gave ourselves."

Sad, Cate thought. *But then they're orphans. Maybe the people who ran the place didn't know their real names.* When she asked where they lived, the children looked at one another and shrugged.

Prissy replied, "We just...*are*, I guess."

Elva, the youngest, cried, "I can show you where we used to live. Wanna see?"

"No!" Marnie admonished, pinching Elva on the arm until she cried. "You can't take her there. It's not allowed."

"She's nice, and I want to show her how I looked...before. I'm not ashamed."

"It ain't pretty."

"I don't care. Come with me, Cate." The little girl held out her hand, yearning for a mother's touch, but Cate's hand slid right through it. Denied the intimacy she craved, a tear ran down the ghost child's spectral cheek.

"I'm going with her," she said to Phil. He insisted on coming along, but this was something Cate felt she should do alone. "I'll meet you in the front room when we're finished," she said, following Elva into the hallway. Phil convinced her they should capture everything that happened on camera and tagged along behind her.

Thinking how bizarre it was to be following a ghost down a hallway, Cate asked, "Are we going to a cemetery?"

"A *ceme-tery*? I never heard that word. I'm taking you to where we all used to live." Cate and Phil followed the ghost child up the stairs and along the second-floor hallway. Elva stopped in front of a half-sized door and said, "You can't always see this door. He makes it appear, and that means he's around somewhere."

"What do you mean?" Cate asked, thinking how much the strange door, out of place among the others that lined the hallway, resembled the one Alice had to pass through to get to Wonderland.

Without replying, the ghost glided through it. Cate tried the knob, found it locked, and called out, "Elva honey, I can't come with you," and the specter reappeared in the hall.

"I forgot you can't do what I do." Elva chuckled as she pointed to the rotting carpet runner on which Cate stood. "He always kept the key under there."

"Who is he? Who are you talking about?" Cate asked as she knelt, ran her hands under the carpet, and brought out a skeleton key.

"The bad man. Do you know him?"

"No. What's his name?"

"We're not allowed to say it." The wispy ghost turned and pointed to the lock. Cate inserted the key, turned it, and pulled the door. After a couple of tugs, it creaked open with a ghastly moan, revealing what had once been a large bedroom. Rotting remains of flimsy cots lined the walls, and as she and Phil stepped inside, A sense of mourning overcame Cate as she thought of the years of fear, neglect and hurt that had happened inside this room.

"This place…this was your bedroom?"

Elva hovered over one of the collapsed beds and pointed. "I lived here. This one is mine."

"I don't understand. You *lived* in this house…"

"I lived in this *room*. We all did. And we're all still

here, kind of."

Confused, Cate told Elva she didn't understand. The little spirit glided to another spot. She extended a trembling hand and pointed toward the wooden floorboards beneath her feet. Cate shrugged off the shiver that ran down her spine, realizing there was much more to this revelation.

The boards appeared worn and loose, and a sense of dread settled over her as she summoned the courage to press on.

"I'm down there. Under those floorboards."

"Oh! Oh, my God, Elva! Your...uh, your earthly body is under the floor?"

"All of us. We're all under there."

Overcome with emotion, Cate reached for a loose board so rotten that she easily pried it out. She tried another, then a third. With each creaking board she lifted, her breath caught in her throat. What lay below was a chilling, ghastly sight—the remains of little ones in tattered dresses, their forms contorted in agony. Some were reaching out...*dear God*, she whispered as the weight of the tragedy became clearer. The faces of those lost souls were etched with fear and despair.

Tears welled up in her eyes, as she voiced her thoughts. "You were trapped inside this room. And when you died, someone buried your little bodies under the floor, while the ones still alive went on living in the room above."

Which one is you, Elva? Cate thought, and the ghost child heard. She pointed to a child lying peacefully as if asleep, sandwiched in between two other little bodies.

Thank God you're not one of the tormented ones.

"Some of them weren't quite dead," Elva whispered. "Them's the saddest ones. They cried a lot until they died."

Cate knelt, looking into the communal grave as her heart ached for the pain they endured, especially the ones who'd been buried alive. "How...how did you die?" she asked.

Elva cocked her head and thought for a moment. "They locked us up one day and never brought any food or water. I got really tired, and I lay down. Next thing I know, I was like this, looking down at what I used to be."

"How many of you are there?"

"Eighty," the child answered. "There are eighty of us trapped here. We can't leave this place until he lets us and until we find peace."

"I promise I will help you find peace," she said. "I'm not sure how, but I will figure something out. You children have suffered enough; no one deserves this."

The ghost's eyes seemed to express gratitude, and as she nodded, she looked past Cate toward the door and vanished in an instant. Cate heard a rustle and looked behind her to see a very tall man wearing a black robe standing in the doorway. He laughed—a drawn-out, feral sound—and asked how she expected to help the children find peace when she herself was now his captive. Concentrating on her, the figure ignored Phil, who kept filming from a far corner.

The intense hatred she felt for this beast, surely the "bad man" who imprisoned these foundlings, overpowered her fears and sense of reason. She jumped to her feet and cried, "Who are you? What kind of creature could do these things? They're *children*, for God's sake…"

Another harsh, humorless laugh. "Invoking your god is fruitless, Miss Adams. In this house you are among true deities, the rulers of heaven and earth. About the children— what of them? They led miserable, pointless lives, and then they died. Their fate is none of your concern, and your fury is misdirected. I bear no responsibility for their deaths; they were entombed by another."

"Bezaliel, I suppose. I don't believe you. You were involved too. You lived here and could have stopped this horror. Look at the bodies; some of them were buried alive!" She pointed at the makeshift graveyard under the floorboards. "Look at them! Take responsibility for what you and Bezaliel did to these poor waifs!"

His piercing eyes never left her face. "Why should I? What is done is done. You should be concerned about the irreversible course your companions have embarked upon. Your thoughts should be directed at convincing the others to refrain from meddling in things they will never understand. If they persist, each of you will meet your doom within these haunted walls after suffering torment so excruciating that you will cry out for death to free you." He ducked his head to waddle through the small door and closed it. She heard the key turn in the lock.

Phil ran to her side as she moaned, "Phil! Phil, I can't bear to be in this room a moment longer! The grief, the thought of all these wasted lives, the horror of children buried alive—get me out of here. I can't take it!" She fell to the grimy floor and cried.

CHAPTER THIRTY-SIX

Phil tried the doorknob, but it wouldn't budge. "We have to call for help," he said, taking out his phone, but before he could press a button, Cate cried, "Wait. Look at this!"

A mist formed in the room, twirling and turning before molding into translucent figures. Ghost children appeared one by one until they filled the room. They watched in silence until Cate mustered her strength and said, "Please help us find a way out of here."

Marnie, the oldest of the three ghosts who had spoken to Cate downstairs, replied, "I told Elva not to bring you here, but there's a way to get out. The bad man put the key back under the carpet. Slide something under the door and hook it, and you can bring it into this room."

Phil looked through the camera case he always carried and pulled out a set of aluminum extension camera poles. "One of these might work," he said, dropping to the floor and peering under the door as best he could while extending the stick. Just then, Marnie passed through the door and guided him from the other side.

"Left. Left a little more. You're there. Nope, you

moved it. A little to the right."

The maneuvering went on for several minutes, and at last she told Phil he'd snagged the key. "Take it slow," she said as he pulled the pole carefully back inside the room. At last he saw the key, grabbed it, and thanked the specter for her help.

They emerged into the empty hallway, went downstairs into the dining room, and Cate assured the children she and her friends were working hard on a plan to stop Bezaliel and Proteus and free them at last. Then she and Phil returned to the office to confess where they'd been and reveal the horrendous truth they'd learned about where the orphans were buried.

CHAPTER THIRTY-SEVEN

Henri and Landry barely glanced their way as Cate and Phil walked in, since they thought the two had had a long lunch and a car repair appointment. A few minutes later, after they contritely offered confessions and said how grateful they were to be free, Landry accepted their apologies. He knew how terrifying it felt to be locked up there, and he had experience with fibbing about his plans, getting into trouble, and having to eat crow later.

Phil became hero of the day, having kept his camera running to capture everything they saw—the disappearing door in the upstairs hall, the bodies buried under the floorboards, and Proteus Moro's threatening tirade against Cate. Proteus looked the epitome of evil, and if Tartarus House ever became the subject of a *Bayou Hauntings* episode, this footage would help set the tone.

Before they watched the video, Landry had invited Jack to join them. He declined, and it pained him to miss the meeting. He wanted to see what had happened, but instead he was sitting at his desk at Channel Nine a few blocks away.

From the day Landry left WCCY-TV and Jack assumed

Landry's senior position, the station manager had cautioned Jack against the appearance of impropriety by spending too much time with his old friend and mentor. He needed to be his own man, find his own news stories, and ensure no one considered him Landry Drake's puppet.

"Develop leads on your own and don't tag along when Landry comes up with something new," Ted Carpenter had advised, and when Jack related the conversation, Landry understood. Both were close friends of Ted's, but as station manager, it was his job to foster and guide his own employees, not devote time or energy to ones who jumped ship to form a new cable network.

They also invited Madame Blue to come over, but she declined, saying she was hard at work on the plan to stop the Harbingers. Cate offered to narrate the video if the psychic would stay on the phone, so she did.

Still shaken from her experience, Cate described how the half-door in the hallway wasn't always visible and talked about Elva, the ghostly child who showed them the bodies under the floor in that sparse room where the orphans lived. She described the tiny corpses, the agony on some of their faces, and her despair at their plight. She had become paralyzed with fear as Proteus made his demands and locked them in that room, which bore such an imprint of sadness and loss.

She explained how the ghost-child Marnie had facilitated their escape, and then turned back to the beings in the house. "We can't go back without a plan," she said. "Madame Blue, I hope you can develop a plan in time."

Cate's voice dropped to a whisper as she added, "How can we free those poor, tormented children? Their little souls cry out for peace."

Madame Blue spoke for the first time since the video had begun. "Listen to me, Cate. Please don't think me callous, but he can no longer hurt them. Possibly we can help them later, but for now our only concern must be the danger that faces our city. In recent days, people in New Orleans have died at the hands of these demons, and as I mentioned, we too will feel their wrath unless we chart our course with the utmost care. Our immediate goal is to learn what he wants. The book, of course, but what's his purpose for continuing the Harbingers? Is a day of reckoning coming a few days from now on Mardi Gras? What torment will he unleash upon others to further his aims, and do we have the power to stop him?"

Those questions burned in the minds of Landry and his friends, and their hearts were heavy with the burden they carried. It appeared more and more likely that if New Orleans was to be saved, it would be because of their efforts. As of now, they had no way of making that happen.

CHAPTER THIRTY-EIGHT

In most years Carnival in New Orleans—the days leading up to Mardi Gras—was a crazy, busy, profitable time for locals. Hotels were full, fine restaurant dining was impossible without a reservation made months earlier, and venues along Bourbon, Decatur and Frenchmen Streets were packed with visitors enjoying authentic Cajun-style music.

This year, because of the Harbingers, a dark cloud of fear overshadowed the once-lively atmosphere of the Mardi Gras season. For the past week, the city held its collective breath as it waited for the next awful thing to happen. The authorities were as baffled as the residents; no one knew the origin of the entity that was behind the Harbingers nor its intentions, but as one day of horror led to another, people became too scared to carry on. No one knew where or what time of day death and destruction would strike next, and as news spread of the gruesome execution at a French Quarter Mardi Gras party on Wednesday night, thousands—residents and visitors alike—called it quits. New Orleans was no fun anymore. Instead of revelry, everyone spoke of ghosts and the supernatural and impending doom.

On Thursday morning before news of Wednesday's horrific tragedy spread, many shops had opened as usual. The parades ran on schedule, but by the afternoon almost every store was shuttered. Once word spread, the customers vanished, locals huddled at home behind locked doors, and everyone who wasn't permanent began getting the hell out of Dodge.

Thousands of tourists abandoned New Orleans, losing five-night-minimum prepaid rooms at upscale hotels and incurring steep fees for changing airline tickets. The ones who'd driven crowded onto Interstate 10, and reporters in news helicopters filming bumper-to-bumper traffic in the outbound lanes harked back to the rush to escape Hurricane Katrina back in 2005.

The bells in the cathedral on Jackson Square tolled the hour of midnight, echoing through empty streets in the Quarter, and local television stations interrupted late-night programming to advise a milestone had been reached: a day passed without one of the terrifying Harbingers. On Thursday, five days before Fat Tuesday, nothing awful had happened.

On Friday, the city was like a morgue. Streets that earlier in the week bustled with activity stood eerily quiet. Loud music blared from a half-dozen bars on Bourbon Street, but most were padlocked. Everywhere one looked—Galatoire's, Arnaud's, Desire, GW Fins—signs in the windows read CLOSED UNTIL FURTHER NOTICE.

Trying to maintain a shred of normalcy, two parades limped down their routes, and the handful of spectators were rewarded with dozens upon dozens of beads and trinkets the krewe members had purchased. As the hours counted down and night fell on the French Quarter, people who lived there hunkered down indoors, leaving no one to stroll down Bourbon or Royal or Decatur. Café du Monde remained open, but few tables were occupied, whereas at any other time during Mardi Gras season, there would have been a line of people out the door.

For a second night, the city was quiet. The Harbingers didn't strike the French Quarter, and the people breathed a collective sigh of relief.

Saturday morning dawned bright and so did the hearts of the people as they gave normalcy a tentative try. Almost every establishment opened for business, street bands and impromptu parades snaked through crowds on the narrow streets of the Quarter, and many tourists who'd left—those living close enough to make an easy drive back—returned to reoccupy their paid-for rooms and honor their hard-earned restaurant reservations. At noon, after two days dark, the steamboat *Jeff Davis* restarted its three-hour rides along the Mississippi River as servers in white jackets served tourists twelve-dollar cups of cheap Chardonnay while the steam calliope whistled "When the Saints Go Marchin' In."

The signature event of the day—the thing that Orleanians would look back upon as the final straw—took place Saturday evening on that famous old steamboat. The sky was streaked with gold as the *Jeff Davis* pulled away from the St. Ann Street dock and floated downriver on its signature three-hour Creole Cocktail Cruise. A Dixieland trio played requests as the sun set on downtown New Orleans. Tourists on the top deck waved to barge and tugboat captains as they passed by heading upriver, and every person on board, from the captain to the servers in the restaurant to the six hundred and twenty-two passengers, breathed a sigh of relief. This was how the days leading up to Mardi Gras were supposed to be—calm, filled with laughter and music and dancing—and nothing could interrupt the reverie of this splendid trip on a beautiful old steamboat.

In interviews afterwards, several people who happened to be at the stern on the open-air upper deck gave similar reports about what happened at 8:18 p.m., as dusk settled over the mighty river. Far behind the boat, a hundred feet or so above the Mississippi, something large and ominous approached out of the darkness, moving in their direction. As it drew closer, a few cries of alarm rang out from those watching it, and within seconds, once they could see how enormous the thing was, people screamed, "Run! Dear God, run!!"

Many of the guests had signed up for dinner or a wine tasting, and they were down inside the ship on the first and second decks. Only a couple of hundred remained topside, and they would be the ones who witnessed something too spine-chilling to believe. A monstrous flying creature approached the stern of the boat and dropped from the sky. Its massive wingspan stretched nearly thirty feet from tip to tip, and its sinuous body was covered in shifting, glistening scales, shimmering in shades of deep midnight blue and iridescent green. The creature's eyes glowed bright red, piercing the darkness, and as it glided slowly and silently from stern to bow, it opened its enormous jaws to reveal razor-sharp fangs extending from a ghastly beak that was both bird's bill and serpent's mouth. It was a thing of legend that tonight had become an undeniable, horrific reality.

Halfway down the length of the riverboat, it appeared to notice the screaming people for the first time. Its eyes gleamed with anticipation as it descended, extending its spindly legs and flexing its dagger-like talons. While the guests scrambled to get out of its path, the giant beast snatched two of them—an older woman and a young man—then flapped its massive wings and rose into the sky.

In a bizarre cacophony of noises, the calliope continued to belt out Dixieland music while the captives screamed in horror as they were lifted into the air. The creature turned its massive head, looked back at the boat, and uttered a piercing shriek that sent a shudder of panic through the crowds. Fearful of its return, screaming, blubbering people stumbled over each other, scrambling for the stairwells to flee the upper deck and find safety inside the ship. In the resulting melee, twenty-nine people would be crushed to death.

Those still on the top deck saw the creature fly away, its scales shining in the moonlight. Some would later describe it as a thing of folklore or nightmares—something unreal while tangible enough to grab two unsuspecting people, neither of whom would be seen again.

"It was the most terrifying thing I've ever experienced," a thirty-something girl from New Jersey would tell reporters. "Everything played out in less than a minute, and the monster was something you couldn't conjure up in your wildest imagination, but it was all real. I saw it, and I'll never, ever be the same."

CHAPTER THIRTY-NINE

The terrifying events on the riverboat were the tipping point—the final nail in the coffin, some chuckled grimly. The attack crushed the resiliency of even the most hard-core, dedicated residents and visitors. On any other midnight during Carnival season, the revelry would be in full swing as thousands of people crammed the streets of the French Quarter, eating, drinking and carousing. But at that midnight on that unforgettable Saturday, everyone's thoughts were on a mythical creature that had swept from the sky and snatched up two unsuspecting tourists from the riverboat *Jeff Davis* as the famous sternwheeler meandered along the Mississippi.

The boat docked at St. Ann Street. As hundreds of people rushed down the gangplank, they were bombarded by news teams, and the word spread quickly. This Harbinger was the most bizarre and terrifying yet: two tourists snatched up by a prehistoric bird, many others dead on the ship, and hundreds of eyewitnesses reduced to babbling, bawling people whose minds couldn't process what their eyes had seen. Everyone knew that something in this city was frightfully wrong. The Harbingers were becoming increasingly deadly, and no one dared to stay around for the next tragedy.

On Sunday the streets were empty. No diehard shopkeepers swept their sidewalks, no intrepid tourists went searching for coffee and beignets, and the interstate highways were clogged like never before. Nobody could take any more of this, and the city sat in desolation. On wrought-iron balconies overlooking Bourbon Street, once-colorful decorations of purple, green and gold hung limp, and the music that had echoed through the streets was replaced by an eerie silence.

By daylight a decision had been made to cancel the extravagant Mardi Gras parades scheduled for Sunday afternoon. Krewe members were no longer interested in riding on the floats, and revelers didn't have the heart—or the nerve—to stand on the sidewalks trying to catch beads and doubloons when something awful might happen. St. Charles Avenue, the route for the biggest parades, ordinarily would have been lined with folding chairs set out by families who would watch the beautiful floats pass by. Instead, homeowners on ladders were removing the fancy Mardi Gras decorations that had adorned their beautiful antebellum mansions. The biggest day of Carnival was still two days off, but for everyone in New Orleans, enough was enough. The partying and festivities were over.

Landry, Cate and Henri sat in the courtyard of Henri's building. Like most every other business, the owner of the brewpub that leased the space hadn't bothered to open, so instead of placing an order, they drank coffee Cate brought from home in a thermos. She commented on how tragic it was that the Harbingers seemed to have brought Mardi Gras to a halt, and so far the people had no inkling who was responsible or why.

But they knew, and they nodded when Henri interjected, "By now there's no question who's behind the supernatural events." Although Bezaliel and Proteus Moros had apparently used the portal to come to New Orleans centuries earlier, their being a part of the Harbingers was irrefutable by now, although Landry and his friends still couldn't fathom the reasons.

"We must learn what they want," Landry said. "If we can give it to them, we do it. If we can't, then we fight until we force them back to whatever pit they crawled out of."

Henri shook his head. "That's an optimistic statement, but it's impossible. I don't think we *can* beat them. Let's call Madame Blue. The other day she told us she was working on a plan, and maybe she can tell us what to do." They agreed, Henri called her, and as always these days, she came right over.

They moved upstairs and sat around the conference table. The psychic quipped, "Your office is considerably quieter than it's been the past several days. All the people who wanted answers got something else instead. They got scared out of their wits and left town."

"Isn't it a tragic situation we're facing?" Henri replied. "Which brings us to our reason for calling. You mentioned you were working on a plan to stop Bezaliel and Proteus and free the spirits of the children. Since then, a giant flying reptile attacked the riverboat last night. This madness can't continue. We must try to stop it, I'm not sure anyone else can, and perhaps it's futile for us to try as well. Frankly, I don't know where to begin. I'm hoping—as are we all—that you've come up with something."

She nodded. "Presuming his goal was to disrupt Carnival completely, Bezaliel has accomplished what he intended. After enduring his shenanigans, all we know for certain is that he wants one of the books Cate found. I've explained that book contains secrets that could give him unfathomable power. Knowing that he could use it for even greater harm, we cannot allow him to have it. Instead, I am reading it, hoping to find a spell or a secret that will harness his destruction and banish him from Earth. It's a slow process, the book has brittle pages, and many are missing. It is in Latin and requires careful translation, and there are hundreds of lines of text. I had hoped to be further along, but I've only examined perhaps a quarter of the book, and meanwhile Bezaliel and Proteus have brought Mardi Gras to a halt."

She cautioned Henri, Cate and Landry about challenging Bezaliel and Proteus without having a workable plan, reminding them they couldn't fathom the risks involved. "I've explained those two aren't mortals. Are they the ancient Greek gods whose names they carry, or are they something straight from Hell? They use the last name Moros, the spirit of impending doom. Gods don't take surnames, but to adapt in modern society, they had to do so. Why did they choose Moros? Because it epitomizes the pure evil that exists in them. Each of us has witnessed what they can do, our quiet city is a testimony to their supernatural power, and I can't describe the danger you may find yourselves in if you confront them.

"I'm working on a strategy to confront the deadly threat posed by those two monsters. Each of us will have responsibilities, and the long-forgotten artifacts Cate found will be our tools and guides. We are the last bastion of defense against Bezaliel and Proteus; I am convinced they intend to destroy our beloved city and the people who call it home. We must fight them, even if one or more of our group gives his life in the battle.

"I'm going now. Time is short, and tomorrow I will be ready. I will instruct you on the use of the magic talismans, and I will inform you what role each will play. Then we will face our adversaries and our destinies."

CHAPTER FORTY

Lundi Gras, or "Fat Monday," was the day before Mardi Gras. At one time a day of rest before the festivities on Tuesday, it had evolved into just another day of raucous celebration, excessive eating and drinking, and downtown parades more spectacular and colorful than the previous ones. Parades were symbols of joy and community, embodying the spirit of Carnival and giving tourists an unforgettable experience.

Fat Monday was a bust this year, of course, because the Harbingers put an end to parades, joy, Carnival and tourism. After a Sunday on which even the hardiest souls admitted defeat, there would be no celebrating on Lundi Gras.

Over twenty-four hours had passed since the attack on the riverboat *Jeff Davis*, and Sunday passed without incident. "I don't think it's that surprising," Landry said to his five friends gathered in his conference room. "If Bezaliel's goal was to ruin Carnival and scare everyone off, he did one hell of a job. The place is a ghost town."

As the mayor and city officials struggled to come up with any solution except total lockdown, these six people at the Paranormal Network were completing preparations to rid New Orleans of Bezaliel and Proteus Moros. Landry, Cate, Henri and Jack Blair listened as Madame Blue stood before them, enumerating bullet points on a whiteboard. Places. Responsibilities. Equipment check. Script memorization. Fallbacks. Worst-case scenarios. From the back of the room, Phil Vandegriff memorialized everything.

Each of them held one of the five magical objects from the wooden box Cate found in the secret room. Madame Blue assumed the role of instructor, spending individual time with the crew until each understood the purpose of their object and how to use it. With one exception, she intended to unleash each object's power herself, but others had to be prepared to take over if Bezaliel struck her down.

The seeress worried whether the mysterious objects would work. They seemed authentic, and she had done exhaustive research on them, but she'd only seen one in action, when she'd read Cate's thoughts about giving Bezaliel the book he demanded. Their only hope was to follow the instructions to the letter. And pray.

Madame Blue thought the two ancient books would give them leverage. She had studied them—a book of spells and incantations, and a book of powerful arcane knowledge—and both rested inside her backpack. She intended to keep them safe, but if literal hell broke loose when they confronted the immortals, they might become bargaining chips to save lives.

The seeress had insisted they make their move tonight, on the eve of Mardi Gras day, and that insistence was based on an educated guess. There had been no parades yesterday, and today's were cancelled as well, but the psychic had a theory that something unusual would happen at five this afternoon. Despite everything, she thought the second-oldest Mardi Gras parade might just roll into downtown.

The Krewe of Proteus, a sea god who could tell the future and change shapes at will, had been in existence since 1882. Its flamboyant procession of floats, bands, clowns and flambeau carriers marched every Lundi Gras night, and Madame Blue had built her plans on the theory that Moros would use his son Proteus's namesake parade to create the greatest scene of chaos yet. The parade had been cancelled, and no police barricades had been erected along the route, nor would cops maintain order in the streets. No dignitaries would be in the viewing stand outside Gallier Hall to welcome King Proteus, and no TV personalities from the national networks would broadcast the festivities.

But although the streets would be empty and the floats devoid of krewe members throwing beads, Madame Blue's belief that the Proteus parade would appear was far more than a hunch. Through her power of mediumship, she could communicate with the spirit world, and she had particular entities in that realm to which she turned for advice about the future. In this instance, she had asked for guidance about a catastrophe that would occur on one of the last two days of Carnival.

Her spirits confirmed her fears were real—an event of great magnitude was indeed set to occur unless it was somehow thwarted. But the exact time and place were a mystery. The entities from the otherworld couldn't tell her enough, and Madame Blue believed she knew why. Her adversaries—two powerful supernatural beings capable of thwarting the efforts of mortals and the spirit world alike—had kept a lid on their specific plans.

Her skills of extrasensory perception and mediumship were unsurpassed, and she had employed every means to divine the future, but the details of Bezaliel's plans remained uncertain, so Madame Blue had to take a chance. If she was correct, tonight the king of Proteus wouldn't be the local dignitary who'd been elected to the position a year ago. Instead, the king would be the real thing—the manifestation of the god Proteus, riding with his father in a ghostly procession of floats.

Today, as Madame Blue coached the team and listened to each enumerate the responsibilities she had assigned them, she believed they had done all that was possible. The plan was risky, and everything had to fall into place in perfect sequence. Their minds had to remain clear so they could rely on her spells, keeping the immortal fiends from discerning their thoughts.

Everything hinged on one supposition, her belief that the parade would somehow roll tonight. If it didn't—if the beings were inside Tartarus House—they would be caught red-handed and lose their lives.

Of the six huddled around the conference table, one would remain behind—Jack Blair. If things went awry, someone had to tell the world what happened. The others—Landry, Henri, Cate and Phil—would be with Madame Blue, each implementing their part of the plan. Jack would stay at the studio, monitoring their activities through the complex audio and visual equipment Henri would set up throughout the old mansion.

Landry had insisted Cate be the one to stay, but she wouldn't hear of it. "This is the most difficult expedition you've ever been on," she had told him last night as they lay in bed with Simba stretched out between them, snoring softly. "I'll be by your side this time."

"What about him?" Landry choked on the words as he patted the little dog who'd captured their hearts in the short time they'd known him. "Who'll take care of Simba if we don't come back?"

Cate squeezed his hand. "Jack will. I spoke with him about it, and he promised if anything happened to both of us, he'd take our boy. If it came to that, he and Simba would get along fine. I love him too, Landry." That admission led to more tears and the realization that shortly they would face a challenge unlike any other in Landry's career.

As they sat in the conference room, the bells in the cathedral chimed four times, a signal that it was time for action. Madame Blue felt certain even with their powers, Proteus and Bezaliel could not be two places at once. They would be part of the parade, which would start five miles away where all downtown parades began. A typical parade took between three and four hours to finish, so they needed to be at the house on Dauphine Street soon. To be safe, they'd be ready early in case the Moros *père et fils* returned to Tartarus House earlier than expected.

Madame Blue watched each of them examine their equipment before stowing it securely in backpacks and placing the mysterious objects on top. At half past four, Cate and Landry knelt to hug Simba, telling him he had to stay with Jack, and the seeress declared the group as ready as it would ever be. "God willing, we'll do something important before this night is over," she told them as she picked up a pack of her own, and they prepared to leave.

"Or you'll all die trying," Jack murmured, mostly to himself. But the others heard.

CHAPTER FORTY-ONE

It was too late to save Mardi Gras, but the task at hand was far greater. They had to rescue a city and its people. Tartarus House had been ground zero for three centuries—an orphanage from whom no one escaped, the headquarters for a Union general in an occupied city, a portal to the unknown, and a dwelling place for two immortal beings, both hell-bent on making life miserable—or deadly—for everyone in New Orleans.

Phil brought his pickup around to the front of the building, and everyone pitched in to help Henri load eight boxes of equipment into the bed. They squeezed into the cab, and in under five minutes Phil pulled up to the mansion where their well-planned adventure would unfold. Everyone stayed put while Landry got out, stepped through the overgrown yard to the porch, and tried the front doorknob.

Which, to his surprise, turned. He opened the door slightly just to be sure, then left it ajar.

Worried, he mentioned his concern to the others. Why was the door unlocked? Did Bezaliel know their plans, and was this a trick to lure them inside? Or was it nothing to worry about? The beings who occupied the house had no need of doors at all, and perhaps they simply didn't care if it was locked.

Madame Blue was far more concerned about other things that might happen than this, so the group voted to proceed. Landry went back first, stood in the hallway, and cried out, "Bezaliel! Proteus! Show yourselves!" but the house was quiet.

They carried Henri's equipment into the parlor, and he began unpacking and arranging it. Madame Blue motioned for Landry to follow her into the dining room.

"Children," she called gently, "are you here? We need your help."

For a moment nothing happened, but then came rustling sounds and tinkling laughter as the shadowy figures formed in the dark corners of the room. Milky clouds of vapor swept up around the seeress and Landry as three little girls appeared by their sides, hazy and indistinct at first, but soon recognizable as the orphans who had become Cate's friends.

"Where's Cate?" Marnie asked, and Landry called her into the room. The girls grinned, rushed to her, and hugged her legs as best they could with their wispy, ghostly arms.

Cate asked, "Can you help us? We're trying to get rid of the bad men in this house. Are they here?"

"No," the ghost named Prissy replied. "They dematerialized a while ago. It's just us. What do you want us to do?"

Madame Blue wanted to find out where the seat of power lay inside the house—the source of energy that allowed Bezaliel and Proteus to appear as human, to interact with people, and to perform their awful feats of terror. The ghost children didn't understand, so Cate made it into a game.

"Show us the rooms in this house where those bad men live. Where do they stay when they're here, and what do they do? Can you show us that?"

"We sure can!" the youngest child, Elva, chirped. Just then came the crackle of a radio from the parlor. "Two-two-oh, this is dispatch. Respond to call of parade forming at St. Charles and Napoleon. Repeat. Parade forming at St. Charles and Napoleon."

They rushed into the parlor to find Henri fiddling with the dials on the police radio he'd set up. They had brought it so they could learn if Madame Blue's hunch about the Proteus parade was right. The responding officer's voice came across the scanner. "Dispatch, two-two-oh. That can't be right. There haven't been parades for two days. They're all cancelled."

"Roger, two-two-oh. I've gotten fifteen more calls in the past two minutes. There's something happening up there. Resident reports a long row of floats sitting there with nobody on them. All units in the vicinity of St. Charles and Napoleon, respond to multiple calls of illegal parade formation."

"Thank goodness!" Madame Blue cried. "My theory was correct; Bezaliel couldn't resist letting his son become the king of the Proteus parade. Now we can only hope nothing awful happens in the city while it's underway. Let's get moving, folks."

With Bezaliel and Proteus away working their mischief, Henri and Phil placed audio and video recording equipment and dozens of sophisticated sensing devices throughout the first and second floors of the house. The plan called for them to enter the ballroom last, as a team, to minimize the risk of danger to any one of them.

Madame Blue, Cate and Landry hooked two-way radios to their belts and let the trio of spectral girls lead them to the second floor. They followed the ghosts as they went to a door on the left and passed through it. Landry opened the door and found a pitch-black room. They pulled out small, powerful LED flashlights and walked inside.

Landry recalled on the 1755 remodeling plan that all the bedrooms except two had been repurposed as parlors, but this one had no windows. It was small for such a mansion, perhaps eight by ten, and it contained no furniture. In the center of the room was a rectangular stone rising eighteen inches off the floor. It reminded Landry of a bier—the stand used to hold a casket at a funeral—and he asked the children what this room was used for.

"He rests there," Prissy said, pointing to the stone. "The bad man. When he lies on the stone, the room moves around."

"It vibrates," the eldest girl corrected. "He locks the door and orders us not to go through it, but we can feel the room moving."

Madame Blue walked the perimeter, knelt before the stone bier, and examined its base. "This isn't what we're looking for. Are there other rooms that vibrate? Maybe even more than this one?"

"Upstairs," Marnie said, pointing to the ceiling. "That's where both of them spend most of their time."

"In the ballroom?" Landry asked, and the girl nodded. "Can you show us?"

They had agreed not to go to the ballroom except as a group, but Madame Blue's concerns had abated since they knew Bezaliel and Proteus were away. She gave the okay, and the three humans followed the small, wispy shapes that floated up the narrow staircase and through the closed door at the top.

"Let's call Phil," Cate suggested. They waited to ascend until he could join them and begin filming. Once he was ready, they crept up the stairway to the room where Landry had been held.

"The portal is in that room," he said, pointing to another closed door. They walked toward it, but they heard giggling and turned around. The ghost girls were down at the far end of the long ballroom. "Not there!" Elva squealed. "Come over here and look!"

They joined the spirits, who hovered above the floor, pointing at another door. Landry gave it a try, found it locked, and pulled the skeleton keys from his pocket. "I'm glad you thought of everything," he said to Madame Blue, who said she wished it were so, but it remained to be seen if they had the tools they needed.

The door swung open to reveal a shadowy room the size of a walk-in closet. Light flickered off the walls, and they saw a tiny flame emanating from something resting on the floor a few feet away. Madame Blue moved closer, knelt and said, "This is a duplicate of one of the objects Cate discovered in the wooden box. Phil, that was your object to master. Please give it to me."

Phil handed the camera to Landry, removed his backpack, and took out the crystal that burned with perpetual fire. "You'll recall I described its properties of heat, light and healing. But these crystals have another function, as I also stated. They are beacons between realms—guiding lights to help spirits move about the heavens and the earth. And Hell, too. Tartarus is the deepest pit of Hell, where I believe Bezaliel and Proteus ascended from."

She put her own backpack on the floor, took out the book *Secrets of the Ancients*, and flipped through one page after another, whispering, "Hurry! Hurry!" to herself. At last she stopped, mouthed words silently, and said, "Bring the light closer, and give me absolute silence. Children, you as well. I'm going to recite an incantation."

She placed their crystal beside the other one, and as their tiny flames flickered, she uttered words no one understood. Ancient words of magic older than the greatest civilizations on Earth, words that had not been spoken in millennia. As she spoke, her voice grew louder and bolder until she was shouting. The flames grew brighter and stronger, and at last she pointed a finger at them and cried a final word.

Immediately the crystals went dark, and Madame Blue fell backwards, exhausted. Cate rushed to her side, but she shooed her away. "We must hurry! We have only begun our journey. We have closed the door in time and space that allows Bezaliel and Proteus to leave the Earth. Now they are trapped on this side. Come! We have little time to finish the job!"

CHAPTER FORTY-TWO

In the parlor, the police scanner crackled to life every few seconds. Five cop cars had responded to the dispatcher's call to investigate the illegal parade formation. What they found defied belief, and the officers approached cautiously, in case this was the beginning of another Harbinger.

Twenty-two floats sat one behind another, each with a tractor to tug it down the parade route. These were the actual floats of the Proteus parade, although in a phone call, the krewe captain said that wasn't possible. The floats were securely locked in a warehouse across the river in Algiers, where they would sit until next year's Mardi Gras. They couldn't be parked on Napoleon Avenue because nobody had authorized a move, and the members scheduled to ride on the floats had dispersed as soon as the cancellation notice went out. Curious, the krewe captain went to the warehouse, unlocked the doors, and found an astonishing sight. Although security guards had seen no movement, twenty-two floats, each twelve feet high and twenty feet long, were gone. Each had somehow been transported across the Mississippi to the Garden District several miles away.

The cops set up a perimeter and waited, and within an hour they beheld an unbelievable sight. At 5:15, the moment the parade had been scheduled to begin, each of twenty-two tractors started up by itself, engines revving and ready to roll—except that there were no drivers. The massive floats also had no people on them, and the cops watched in astonishment as the handbrake on the first tractor released by itself, and the machine tugged its float around the corner onto St. Charles. The next followed, then the next after that, and the most bizarre parade in history got underway as officers screamed into their radios for backup and orders.

It took almost five minutes for all twenty-two phantom floats to make the turn, and now they were lumbering along toward Lee Circle. With no cops along the route and no barricaded side streets, perplexed drivers navigating St. Charles swerved and veered into the median to get out of the way.

No one knew when the figures appeared on the first float—the one reserved for King Proteus—but once people realized they were there, they watched in stunned silence. One scary figure sat stoically on a gold throne atop King Proteus's float, wearing a black robe and a pointed hat and holding a long wand. The other, similarly dressed but with his face covered by a black cowl, stood behind Proteus.

Residents who lived along the parade route and ventured outside couldn't believe it—a procession rolling by in total silence except for the putt-putting of the driverless tractors pulling each float. No bands, no people tossing beads, no spectators—just a line of unlit floats draped in Mardi Gras purple, green and gold, passing like ghost ships in the night.

Since the Harbingers began, the weather in New Orleans had been dry and warm. It was a perfect week for celebrating Mardi Gras; the late winter to early spring dates when Carnival fell often meant cold, clammy and damp days and nights. But on this balmy evening, the weather took a sudden turn just as the Proteus parade started to move. A chilling wind blew in from the north, and huge thunderclouds appeared in a sky that had been clear moments earlier. As the floats moved along St. Charles Avenue, drops of rain fell, light at first but soon intensifying into a torrential storm.

The weather people would call it a freak event. That was an understatement; there had never been an occurrence like this one. The rainstorm, complete with a blustery wind, flashes of lightning, rolling peals of thunder and driving rain, formed directly above the floats in the Proteus parade, and it stayed above them the entire time they were moving. Elsewhere in the city—even two blocks from the parade route—the sky was clear, and the temperature was around seventy degrees.

The experts couldn't explain it, calling it a previously unknown anomaly created by sudden and unusual weather patterns in the Gulf. But people in the Crescent City didn't believe a word of it. *Just another manifestation of the Harbingers,* they whispered to one another.

CHAPTER FORTY-THREE

The crew returned to the parlor and watched Jack wave to them from a forty-two-inch television screen. "I see and hear everyone loud and clear," he said. "The split screen is working fine on my end."

Everything mechanical was in place and ready to roll. Henri and Phil had rigged the equipment to give Jack a continuous feed from command central—the front parlor—and the audio and video feeds from Phil's portable camera. On another screen, he could view each of twelve small motion-activated cameras positioned throughout the house.

Henri said it was time to set up equipment in the area they considered most critical—the third-floor ballroom. Landry told him what they'd found a few minutes earlier and said he'd accompany them back upstairs to point out the rooms the portal and crystal were in.

An LED clock on the mantel ticked off the seconds and minutes since the parade had begun. This one was lumbering along at the usual pace, and so far, everything was progressing well. They should be ready when the parade ended and the beings presumably would return.

Madame Blue asked Cate to join her on a dusty, tattered

sofa and said, "Give me the dreamcatcher. It's time to find out what Bezaliel truly intends to do." Cate fished the orb from her backpack, watching the mist inside twist and twirl as the seeress held it in her hands.

"Silence for a moment, everyone!" she commanded before closing her eyes to concentrate on her subject and his true thoughts and intentions. Henri shut down all the audio while a minute passed, then another, and at last her eyes popped open, and she stared at them blankly for a few seconds before regaining her composure.

Henri turned the dials, and the police scanner crackled back to life. "Dispatch, parade is approaching Jackson Avenue." Landry glanced at the clock on the mantel; almost ninety minutes had passed, and if things continued without interruption, the parade would end around two hours from now.

That was a big *if*, Landry thought to himself.

"Roger, two-two-oh. Units will block traffic around Lee Circle to avoid potential accidents."

Another unit radioed in. "Dispatch, this is three-one-niner. I'm setting up a barricade at Jackson and St. Charles. Two squad cars will block both lanes to stop the progress."

"Sergeant, who gave you that order?"

"Gotta go, Dispatch. The first float is a hundred yards away."

Everyone but Madame Blue gathered around the scanner to listen for the next report. When it came, it was harsh reality. "This is two-one-five. Oh God, they're on fire! Officers down! Officers down! Get backup and ambulances and fire units. Jackson and St. Charles. Repeat, Jackson and St. Charles!"

The psychic sat on the couch with the dreamcatcher orb still in her hands. Her eyes were closed once again, and she rocked back and forth as she began speaking in a deep, guttural voice.

"You cannot stop me, mortals! Here is your reward for

challenging me!"

Over the next ten minutes they stepped away from their complex plan and listened to police and local radio to learn what had happened. Two police units blocked the street, aiming to force the first float to stop and consequently bring the parade to a halt. But the driverless tractor continued on its way. Thirty feet from an impending collision, the black-robed figure standing atop the float behind Proteus on his throne pointed his wand and uttered words.

Within seconds, the two police cruisers were totally consumed by fire so intense other cops couldn't get near. The first tractor kept moving; as it approached the inferno, the cars inexplicably slid sideways, clearing the road for the parade to proceed in silence. Landry and the others heard sirens and screams for help as the dispatcher warned all units not to engage the phantom parade.

Madame Blue seemed herself once again, and she told them how the dreamcatcher had revealed Bezaliel's thoughts. His power would propel the parade along its route to the end on Tchoupitoulas Street. But as she continued to hold the orb, she revealed even more, as her mind captured Bezaliel's fury that officers would attempt to stop his son's parade.

Four policemen perished in the inferno, two more were injured when the burning cars mysteriously moved and knocked them down, and every officer on the force felt unease and dread because, once again, this was something they had never faced. This was another Harbinger.

"Let's get back on schedule, people," Madame Blue said. "The time is passing quickly, and we must be ready."

CHAPTER FORTY-FOUR

While Henri and Phil set up the remaining devices in the ballroom, a spectral assemblage of perhaps twenty boys and girls floated around the room's perimeter, watching them work. Madame Blue took the tarot cards from Henri, opened the door to the room that held the portal, and stood beside the black square in the floor. She dealt herself one card, then another, and read the Latin phrases each card contained. Curses and blessings, blessings and curses— each designed to protect the five of them and limit the powers of the supernatural beings they would soon face.

Since he was on the top floor, Henri left it to Jack to watch the live TV news footage covering the parade and report anything unusual. Henri's two-way radio squawked as Jack advised it was passing the empty viewing stands at Gallier Hall, and the procession continued without stopping. Henri told the others they had about one hour left.

Madame Blue took stock of the two remaining relics she had at her disposal, the ones she considered most important. She carried the legendary phoenix feather in her backpack; whatever words she wrote with it would create hopes or wishes—or dark curses—that would come true, but at an enormous cost. The more powerful the request, the greater the cost to her, and what she asked would be immensely powerful, which was why she had kept the feather for herself—to ensure the others didn't risk their lives by using it. She possessed vast knowledge of the occult, and she would accept whatever fate awaited her. All she wanted was to stop Bezaliel and Proteus, and to accomplish that goal, she was prepared to sacrifice whatever was required of her.

Landry carried the last object, the beautiful amulet called a Luminarion. Madame Blue's plan was to use the other four objects herself, but the Luminarion was different; the magic amulet created in long-forgotten times was their most powerful tool. She trained Landry on its use because he would be the one to wield the amulet's powers. He would be rendered temporarily invincible, and the ones against whom it was used would be permanently deprived of their very essences, rendering them weak and harmless.

Madame Blue knew from the outset that the final battle, the struggle to take back the city from two ruthless gods from antiquity, could likely result in their defeat. She believed the amulet could be used only once, and they faced two enemies. Could the Luminarion immobilize both Bezaliel and Proteus at once? No one would know until he faced off against them and used the device. She hoped and prayed that Landry could lure them close enough to each other to ensnare both.

She took Landry aside and disclosed her concern that should their plan fail, the city was doomed. Her voice trembled as she spoke words barely above a whisper. "Landry, the gods we're about to face are unlike anything I have ever encountered. They feed on darkness and chaos, and they have snatched away the town's grit and nerve, leaving its citizens cowering behind locked doors in fear. Hurricane Katrina devastated New Orleans, but it survived. This time it may not be so fortunate."

Landry nodded, his expression grave. "That may be true, but you have done all you can to prepare us. You examined the ancient objects Cate found; you learned their purposes and trained us in their uses. You've given us the tools we need, and those are all we have. Three have worked already. You've cast curses and blessings using the tarot cards, and you say the last two relics, the phoenix feather and the Luminarion, are the most powerful of all. We won't know if they work until we try them. I'm scared, Madame Blue. I'm terrified to face Bezaliel and Proteus, but I'm resolved to battle them with every ounce of strength I have."

She squeezed his hand in a rare gesture of warmth. "So am I, Landry. So am I."

The parade turned onto Tchoupitoulas Street, where it would end. As the final float made the turn, each of the driverless tractors shut down. An eerie stillness surrounded the ghostly procession of floats standing like lonely statues in the middle of the street. The phantom parade was over, and the two mysterious figures were gone; as darkness descended on the Crescent City, it was time for an epic confrontation in a mansion on Dauphine Street.

CHAPTER FORTY-FIVE

Landry and the crew formed a circle in the middle of the ballroom to await the imminent return of Bezaliel and Proteus. In a poignant effort to help, the spirits of the orphaned children encircled them, trying in vain to create a protective barrier against the malevolent beings.

A sudden surge of energy rippled through the room, causing Landry's skin to prickle. "Did you feel that?" he asked, and everyone had. A few feet away, the door to the room where the portal lay began to shake, lightly at first but then so violently that it was torn from its hinges and flew past them across the ballroom and slammed into the far wall.

Inside the room, two swirling towers of light materialized, emitting an ominous glow. They watched as the beams twisted and turned before morphing into the creatures they'd been expecting. As Bezaliel and Proteus stepped into the ballroom, the stench of the devil—the now-familiar reek of sulphur—spread through the room.

Bezaliel, a towering figure with crimson eyes and a twisted grin, wielded a staff adorned with vines and thorns. His eyes flickered like burning embers while Proteus, the shape-shifter, changed forms every few seconds, making it impossible to predict his next move. He became a cat, then a giant reptilian creature, then the bloated spider Landry recognized, before returning to his human form.

The gods spoke in chilling unison, their voices echoing throughout the ballroom. "How good of you to assemble in our house. The only people who might have stopped us huddle like terrified lambs before the slaughter." Bezaliel raised his arm, pointed a finger, and shouted, "Children, begone. Now!" As he spoke, a powerful gust of wind arose, and the misty forms of the orphans dissipated in the breeze. Now only three remained—the girls who had become Cate's friends.

"Go, I say!" Bezaliel bellowed. "Get out of my sight, you worthless, irrelevant waifs!" The ghosts vanished.

Cate screamed, "Stop it! Stop calling them names! They've suffered enough."

"Suffered? You know nothing of their suffering. And wait until tomorrow. On Mardi Gras day, everyone brave enough to have stayed in this city will suffer beyond their wildest nightmares. Tomorrow we will unleash chaos upon this city so vast that it will never recover."

"What's the purpose behind all this?" Landry asked Bezaliel. "Why inflict such devastation? This city has been your home for ages."

Towering and ethereal, the god exuded an aura of unearthly power. "My *home* is in Tartarus, not in an earthly house made of bricks and wood. I have *tolerated* this place, but it is time that we return to our own world. And why such devastation? Because we are descended from Moros, the god of impending doom. Mayhem is our destiny. I arrived in this city when it was new, and when I leave, I will destroy it."

His eyes glowed inside twin black holes, sucking in the very essence of the room. With a flick of his hand, Bezaliel summoned a horde of twisted and contorted spectral apparitions that flew through the air, screaming anguished wails as they descended upon Landry. He dodged and ducked as Madame Blue held up a tarot card and read an incantation that dispersed them at once.

"It's time to use the Luminarion," Madame Blue cried. "Remember what I told you, and good luck."

Landry's moment had arrived. He stepped forward, his boots echoing on the wooden floor, reached under his shirt, and removed the amulet from around his neck. As he clasped the ancient device tightly in his hand, its surface burst into a circle of intricate symbols that shimmered and gleamed, each representing a different aspect of protection and control over dark energies. He felt its power surging through his own body and recalled the instructions Madame Blue had drilled into his mind countless times.

Wait until Bezaliel and Proteus are close together and pray that its power will ensnare them both at once. If that doesn't happen, aim for Bezaliel, the most powerful, and with luck, we will find a way to deal with Proteus.

The psychic held more tarot cards in the air, casting curses on the gods and blessings on Landry as he moved to the middle of the room, keeping the Luminarion aimed at the floor while waiting to catch them together. But Proteus was wily, shifting forms rapidly and becoming a menagerie of terrifying creatures both mythological and real, each more formidable than the last. Eight-headed serpentine beasts twisted their awful faces in Landry's direction, but seconds later he faced a gigantic man-eating plant, its deadly trap snapping open and shut as it ducked and weaved.

Hold still just for a moment, Landry ordered the gods in his mind as the shapes continued their bizarre mutations. As fascinating as they were deadly, Landry concentrated on watching Bezaliel, the more dangerous one, and at last the insane shape-shifting paused. Proteus reentered his human form, and Landry raised the Luminarion. As they saw what he was doing, they sneered, their power crackling around them.

Intending to ensnare Landry's mind, Bezaliel lashed out with tendrils of darkness that encircled Landry's head and threatened to engulf him. Landry fought valiantly, but the forces were powerful. Amid shouts and screams from Landry's friends, a creature suddenly bounded into the room from the stairway. Not another malevolent god or multiheaded being, but the fearless dog Simba, who positioned himself between his master and Bezaliel and began barking furiously. Distracted by the dog, the gods paused, and the emanations that had threatened to overwhelm Landry faded. Madame Blue shouted, "Landry, quickly! Use the chant!"

Landry recited an incantation from the *Arcana Antiquorum* book Cate had discovered. The Latin words meant nothing to him, but Madame Blue had practiced with him so many times they had become etched in his memory. While speaking, he raised the Luminarion above his head. It emitted an unearthly bright light, creating a radiant burst of energy that enveloped Landry in a protective aura and empowered him with courage and determination. Instantly the light narrowed into a laser-like beam and hurtled toward the targets—the malevolent, towering god of the underworld and the elusive shape-shifter. The light collided with them both, assuming a palpable form as it swirled around and around like ethereal chains.

With a roar that shattered every window in the room, Bezaliel fought back, writhing and contorting and recoiling against the brilliant light. His son, Proteus, also struggled mightily, attempting to change into something that could escape, but by now the Luminarion had begun unraveling the very fabrics of their existences. As the last vestiges of their powers were drained away, their anguished cries echoed throughout the ballroom.

While Bezaliel and Proteus were reduced to mere

specters, Madame Blue slowly raised her hand, held up a scrap of paper on which words were written, and pointed the phoenix feather at the open door where the portal lay. This was the final touch—the key to stopping the otherworldly beings forever. Her friends watched in silence as she shouted, "Hear my wish! Send these monsters into the portal and seal it behind them, forever banishing them to the underworld."

The air became charged with raw energy. Lightning bolts flashed through the air, and a gale-force wind swept through the ballroom. With a yelp, Simba raced across the room to his master's side, where he continued to growl furiously at Bezaliel and Proteus.

"Stay on your feet!" the seeress cried as the powerful winds threatened to knock them down. As Phil struggled to keep his camera on his shoulder, they linked arms for support and stood firm while watching Bezaliel and Proteus increasingly lose their resistance. Weakened by the searing light's unfaltering assault, at last the Luminarion's magic broke the defenses of the two creatures.

"Lower the amulet!" Madame Blue cried, shouting an incantation that would banish the immortals into the portal that opened to the dark place from which they arose. "Leave this place!" she cried, her voice faltering as the Luminarion's blinding light receded into an afterglow, returning the amulet's crystal to a dormant state.

Bezaliel and Proteus limped away to the safety of the portal. As each stepped into the black square, he was swept down into nothingness. The moment they disappeared, the hole collapsed in on itself, closing the only means they had to return and continue the mayhem. This had been the coup de grâce; Madame Blue's wish written with a phoenix feather had saved the day.

Realizing the trick that had been played upon them, the two gods shouted and cursed from beneath the floor, striking the boards over and over in a vain attempt to reopen the portal and finish the battle. But the powers of the objects used against them had proven too potent, and moments later they were gone.

A cheer went up from the victors as they high-fived and slapped Landry's back amid the echoes of a triumphant battle. As Madame Blue had predicted, the ancient Luminarion proved itself an artifact capable of conquering even the darkest of deities. And the phoenix feather had granted her wish.

Landry felt as if the world's troubles had been lifted from his shoulders, and as he turned to thank the psychic for making it happen, he heard the ghostly children crying. "Oh no! Oh no!" their tinkling, ethereal voices wailed as they huddled in a swirling mass a few feet away.

"What are you doing?" Landry shouted, and the children parted to reveal Madame Blue, who lay on the floor, unmoving.

The woman who had guided them, who had interpreted the meaning of the ancient books and objects Cate found, who had imparted her knowledge and instructed them so perfectly that they won the battle, was dead. Although each was deeply saddened, none was surprised, since Madame Blue had prepared them for this possibility. She had explained that the more powerful the request written with the phoenix feather quill, the higher the cost to the one writing it. She had asked for the portal to close forever, and in exchange for a wish granted, she willingly paid the ultimate price.

CHAPTER FORTY-SIX

After they left Tartarus House, Henri called the mayor, who threw together a press conference that made the ten o'clock news. In no other city could a leader explain with a straight face how supernatural forces that disrupted Mardi Gras were defeated by a ghost hunter and his team, who banished the beings to the underworld. Anywhere else he'd be called crazy, but this was New Orleans, a haunted town with a series of Harbingers that had almost brought it down. Now the horror was over.

The mayor also offered his condolences at the death of Madame Blue, who gave her life to save the city, adding that he regretted it was too late for the biggest Mardi Gras parades of all to roll out tomorrow on Mardi Gras day. They would have served as a fitting honor both to the seeress and to the resilience of the city of New Orleans.

At 10:30 p.m., following the mayor's announcement, Channel Nine aired a quickly arranged sixty-minute show that topped the ratings. Jack Blair gave a firsthand account of how two mythological beings carried out a reign of terror from Tartarus House in the 800 block of Dauphine Street. The Harbingers were over, thanks to paranormal investigator Landry Drake and a team of compatriots who faced the otherworldly beings and bested them in battle. Jack had watched it all happen, and thanks to footage Phil had rushed to piece together, viewers had an unprecedented opportunity to watch the supernatural in real life. A crawler at the bottom of the screen reminded them that the broadcast contained violent scenes unfit for children, and that everything they were seeing was real. Following Landry's order, Jack mentioned nothing about the five mysterious objects or the ancient books, nor did video footage show them in use.

Jack's newscast included a stirring eulogy honoring Madame Blue, the noted psychic and seeress who'd been a fixture in New Orleans for decades, and who correctly interpreted the meanings and uses of five ancient relics found in the haunted building that housed Landry's Paranormal Network. A valiant and dedicated student of the occult, the seeress stood alone among the pretenders who read palms and told fortunes for tourists. She had faced the enemy and given her own life to rescue her beloved city and its people from the scourge that befell them during Carnival.

Jack ended his special broadcast with a tantalizing announcement—in a few months, Landry's Paranormal Network would release a two-hour presentation called "Dread Reckoning" that would provide much more detail, and thanks to the hours of video Phil had captured, viewers would experience the same horrors and frightful encounters as Landry's team.

After the broadcast, Landry sent Jack a congratulatory text about his newscast, and Jack asked if Simba was okay. He'd realized the dog was missing at some point while Landry and his crew were inside Tartarus House. Landry explained how Simba's diversion had saved the day and allowed Landry to use the ancient curse.

The next morning was Fat Tuesday, Mardi Gras day,

and the city of New Orleans awoke to a new dawn and a fresh beginning. Word had spread that the Harbingers were over, and the streets of the French Quarter were filled with celebratory people laughing, talking and standing in a line that snaked out the door at Café du Monde for chicory coffee and beignets.

Landry and Cate rose with the sun, taking Simba with them. The team had agreed to meet at the office at nine, but they had something to do first. The amulet hung around Landry's neck as they strolled to Dauphine Street and turned the corner, wondering how the little dog would react. But Simba was fine. He trotted briskly beside his master without a fear or a growl until they reached Tartarus House.

The ancient mansion had transformed during the night. The tangled, gnarly yard seemed less unkept, and the gloom that had hung over the house was no more. Now it appeared to be just one more old structure in a town filled with antebellum residences.

Only one task remained unfulfilled today; they walked to the porch, opened the door and stepped inside. The aura of mystery and danger were gone as sunlight streamed through the windows and highlighted dust motes flying everywhere. "Children?" Cate called. "Come here. I have good news for you."

One by one they appeared, eighty in all, their ethereal faces looking up expectantly into hers. The three girls huddled near Cate while other spirit children knelt beside Simba, who gave a little friendly whine to say he didn't understand what ghosts were. When they had all gathered, Cate said, "Listen to me, children. Your tormentors, the gods who have held you captive for so long, have been defeated. They're banished to the dark place from which they came, and they will never return."

The ghosts exchanged hesitant glances, their translucent forms quivering with a mixture of hope and disbelief. "What...what about us?" Marnie asked. "What happens now?"

"You've suffered far too long, but today that suffering ends. We will ensure that your bodies receive proper burials, and as of this moment, your spirits are free at last."

The children formed a line and approached them, passing their transparent hands through theirs. As their hands met, the ghosts felt a surge of peace and warmth they had long ago forgotten. The bond between the ghost hunter and the ghosts grew stronger with each touch. Simba felt it too. His tail wagged, tentatively at first but then enthusiastically as the children knelt to give him a ghostly, translucent pat.

Tears of joy streamed down their spectral faces. Cate cried too as Landry said, "You may go now. Your journey to the afterlife awaits, and there you will find the peace you've been so long denied." His face broke into a smile as he and Cate waved goodbye, watching as they ascended one by one, leaving behind the mansion that had been their prison. At that moment Tartarus House was no longer the most haunted structure in the city.

Before he left, Landry said he had one more thing to do. The three of them went to the ballroom, where he gathered the ancient books and the remaining four relics that lay strewn about the floor and put them in his backpack. Then he opened the door in the closet that held the portal and looked inside.

The floor was smooth and even. There was no black square. And that was exactly what Landry wanted to see. He would later find the same thing had happened at his office. In the hidden room, the black square in the floor had vanished.

They were early for the meeting, so they took Simba to Café Beignet, sat outside with their coffees, and walked to the office to find Henri, Phil and Jack gathered in the conference room. Landry explained where they'd gone.

"We told the children they were free and that we were going to move their bodies from under the floor to a final resting place. I checked out a place that I think would be perfect—the children's burial ground at St. Patrick Cemetery—and I'm going to start the ball rolling on that project tomorrow morning." Cate described being inside Tartarus House, how serene and peaceful it had felt without the malevolent presences, and how the sunlight had come back to that block on Dauphine at last.

When Landry removed the ancient books and the objects from his backpack, Henri smiled and said, "I'm pleased you picked these up. Although it would be a fitting tribute to Jules if they could be displayed at the Cabildo along with a dedication to him, we know how dangerous they could be in the wrong hands. We can discuss it later; for now I'll keep these in my office safe at the Society next door."

"They'll always have to be under lock and key," Cate said. "But maybe with supervision, scholars or researchers could have access to them."

Landry shook his head. "I disagree. We can't reveal that these things exist. It's far too risky, and we don't have Madame Blue to help us decide what to do. No display and no access by anyone, ever. Only we five know about them, and I insist we keep it that way."

Their iPhones dinged in unison, displaying a text from the city's emergency warning system. Instead of another disaster notice, the upbeat message reported that the Krewe of Rex had worked through the night, and the biggest Carnival parade of all would take place after all, assembling in the usual place and rolling out at noon. "The mayor and invited dignitaries will greet King Rex and his entourage at Gallier Hall," the cheery message ended.

"Wow, I'm impressed!" Cate said. "Good for them to make such a huge undertaking happen in just twenty-four hours! After all the fear and terror, it's like a new dawn in the city."

Landry's phone dinged again; he looked at it and said, "Apparently we're dignitaries! The mayor asked us to join him in the reviewing stand."

"Us who?" Phil asked. "I'm no VIP…"

"You are now. What took place last night was a team effort, and we'll all be there to honor Madame Blue's memory and take our bows. I'm proud of what we accomplished, and I'm amazed that it worked like Madame thought it would, so let's go claim our fifteen minutes of fame."

Jack roared with laughter. "Fifteen minutes? Maybe for the rest of us, but you're Landry Drake, ghost hunter extraordinaire and slayer of mythical beings. This is just one more notch in your belt."

"Okay, okay. Whatever. We're to meet in the lobby of Gallier Hall at one."

When it was time, Cate, Landry and Simba walked through the Quarter from their apartment toward the old building in front of which a set of bleachers stood. She had decided to bring the dog along, assuming no one would dare stop them since Simba's father was the famous ghost hunter. People in the streets came up to thank him, and as he reached Canal Street, where hundreds were already staking out their places to watch the upcoming parade, the well-wishers became a mob. As the time to take their places at Gallier Hall drew near, he was stuck amid people wanting handshakes and autographs, and finally Cate broke away and returned with a policeman.

"Move back, folks!" the officer instructed. "Let Mr. Drake through; he's got to meet the mayor at Gallier Hall!" The order worked, and the cop stayed with them until they reached their destination, requested an autograph himself, and then headed back to his post. Cate and Landry walked upstairs, stepped out into the bleachers and took their places alongside Jack, Henri and Phil, who for once was on the receiving end of the cameras.

"The parade is now underway!" the mayor proclaimed as waiters in white jackets passed out mimosas and champagne. Everyone wanted to talk to Landry, and the time passed quickly. They were pleasantly surprised when Angie Bovida stepped into the viewing stand, waved at Jack, and accepted a seat next to him.

"A lot's happened since I was kidnapped ten days ago," she explained. "Who knew what horrible things were in store for this city? I'm just thankful it's all over, and I appreciate the mayor including me in the festivities. What do you think they'll do with that horrible old house? I hope they tear it down!"

Landry said things had changed since the beings were gone. Perhaps it would be condemned and razed, or converted to a museum, or decked out as a grand house once again. The question of ownership would be settled in court, but with no living Moros family members, Landry said he doubted it would be a problem to transfer title if anybody wanted the place.

The long-awaited hour arrived. As the colorful floats came into view, Landry smiled as he watched the spectacle everyone had given up on. The ornate Krewe of Rex floats depicted scenes from the city's history, folklore and diverse traditions, and the crowd celebrated wildly. A rhythm of lively music filled the air as quickly assembled marching bands from local high schools paraded before the dignitaries while dancers wearing vibrant costumes twirled and spun. Krewe members on the floats wore elaborate masks, and there was a sense of camaraderie as the city came together not only to celebrate Mardi Gras but also to commemorate the victory over the forces of evil that had overtaken the populace.

At last the majestic float bearing Rex, King of Carnival, approached the bleachers and stopped to greet the VIPs. Beads and doubloons showered over the attendees as Rex and the mayor raised glasses of champagne in a toast to the future. The procession continued, and as the last float of the parade rounded a corner and disappeared from view, Landry felt a profound sense of accomplishment. Their threat neutralized, the evil gods were banished to Tartarus, and New Orleans had withstood the ultimate test, emerging stronger and more united than ever.

Another commemoration took place later that day. In the kitchen of their apartment, Landry presented Simba a thick bone filled with peanut butter and officially pronounced him a member of the paranormal team. During the mock ceremony, the little dog sat on command and yipped happily when he got his special treat. As he rubbed his friend's head, Landry understood that he had found a helpmate in the most unexpected of companions. He might be an expert in the paranormal, but it took a dog to teach him something new. Now he understood that sometimes the unseen mysteries of the world could be explained with the help of a loyal, four-legged friend.

Thank you for reading *Dread Reckoning.*

If you enjoyed it, I'd appreciate a review on Amazon.
Reviews allow other readers to find books they enjoy, so
thanks in advance for your help.
Please join me on:
Facebook
http://on.fb.me/187NRRP
Twitter
@BThompsonBooks

This is book 9 of the Bayou Hauntings series.
The others are available as paperbacks or ebooks.

MAY WE OFFER YOU A FREE BOOK?
Bill Thompson's award-winning first novel,
The Bethlehem Scroll, **can be yours free.**
Just go to
billthompsonbooks.com
and click "Subscribe."

Once you're on the list, you'll receive advance notice of
future book releases and our newsletter.

Printed in Great Britain
by Amazon